The Living Boat

The Living Boat

The Silent Depths

Book 1

ERIC HAWLEY

The Silent Depths Series

by Eric Hawley

Book One — The Living Boat
A young sailor discovers the heartbeat of the sea and the brotherhood of the boats.

Book Two — Beneath the Rising Sun
As war looms, Mason and the USS *Pike* sail west into uncertainty where calm seas give way to thunder.

More to come.

The Living Boat
Book One of *The Silent Depths Series*
Published by **Silent Service Publishing House**
Snohomish, Washington
ISBN 978-1-970754-00-1 (print)
ISBN 978-1-970754-01-8 (ebook)
Printed in the United States of America
First Edition – December 2025

This story is for you, for every man who took his courage beneath the sea, who served in silence and came back older than his years, and for those who gave their last full measure to the deep.

Contents

Chapter 1
The Living Boat

The wind off the Thames carried the first bite of autumn as Daniel Mason stood in formation on the parade ground at the Submarine School in Groton, Connecticut. Rows of young men in dress blues waited in rigid lines, their white hats square, their polished shoes aligned as perfectly as their training had demanded. Beyond the neat rows of sailors, the river caught the pale morning sun and glittered like a sheet of glass. The air smelled faintly of salt and river mud, of oil from the piers, and of autumn leaves just beginning to turn.

Mason shifted his weight slightly and straightened again. He was seventeen and, though the uniform made him look older, he still felt the farm boy from Illinois under the wool. His parents' faces flickered in his mind, his father's pride, his mother's tears as he boarded the train east months ago. Now he was here, one of the Navy's newest submariners, standing in the cool September air with a diploma waiting in his hands.

The ceremony began with the sound of a small band, their brass catching the sunlight. Flags snapped in the breeze, and the base commander, an older captain with a voice like gravel, reminded them of the burden they had chosen. *"The sea is unforgiving. A boat is not a ship; it does not grant you space or mercy. You will live by inches and seconds. Respect your boat, and respect each other, or you will not live at all."*

Mason swallowed hard. He thought of the long days and nights of training. The escape tank that great steel tower that swallowed recruits whole, flooding in a rush until you kicked upward through a column of cold water, lungs burning and ears screaming as you trusted the thin hiss of the Momsen lung to keep you alive. How his chest had burned as he kicked for the top, the darkness around him pressing close. The flooding trainer, when water rushed in faster than he could think, and he had to trust his partner's hands in the dark. The first dive in a real submarine, when the world tilted and the deck hummed underfoot as the sea closed over them.

The commanding officer's words blurred in his ears. Mason's heart thudded. He was proud, but nervous. This wasn't a game anymore.

One by one, the graduates stepped forward to receive their certificates and orders. When Mason's turn came, the yeoman read them aloud: *"Report to Submarine Base, San Diego, California. Assignment: USS Pike, SS-173."*

Mason blinked. *Pike.* He had never heard the name before, but it sounded sharp, dangerous. He imagined a sleek predator of the deep, waiting for him on the far coast. He tucked the papers carefully into his pocket and stepped back into formation.

When the ceremony ended, the class broke apart in a sudden rush of voices. Some slapped each other on the shoulders, promising to write, others already tearing open their orders. Mason compared notes with two of his classmates.

"Pearl Harbor for me," said O'Malley, a broad-shouldered Irish kid from Boston. He grinned. "Imagine that, Hawaii. Palm trees, hula skirts, the works."

"Panama Canal for me," said Jones, wiry and dark-eyed. "Assigned to an S-boat down there. Guess I'll be sweating my hide off."

Mason held up his orders. "San Diego. USS *Pike*."

Neither of them recognized the name either, but O'Malley clapped him on the back. "West Coast. That's still better than a swamp in Panama."

They laughed, though it felt brittle. Beneath the humor, they all knew this was goodbye. The Navy scattered them across the oceans, and who knew when, if ever, they would meet again.

The New London station was crowded, noisy, and full of smoke. Mason stood with his seabag slung across his shoulder, waiting for the westbound train. Around him, classmates said hurried goodbyes, some shaking hands, others hugging in quick, embarrassed bursts of affection.

O'Malley gave him one last grin. "Good luck, Mason. Don't let that *Pike* chew you up."

"You too. Watch out for those hula girls," Mason shot back, and then the train whistle blew, and it was time.

He climbed aboard, stowed his bag in the overhead rack, and then found a nearby seat by the window. The engine shrieked, the cars lurched, and New London slid away behind him.

The countryside rushed past: small Connecticut towns with white church steeples, red barns nestled in valleys, rivers winding between hills glowing with russet leaves. The air wasn't snowy yet, but it carried the crisp tang of coming winter. Mason pressed his forehead to the glass and let the rhythm of the wheels soothe him.

The first days blurred together. The train thundered through New York, past factory towns with tall smokestacks, then west into Pennsylvania. He saw men in threadbare coats waiting in bread lines, women selling apples on street corners. The Depression still lingered in every tired face.

At station stops he bought coffee and sandwiches from vendors. Once he struck up conversation with an older chief in worn khakis who was bound for Mare Island. The man studied Mason's fresh blues with a crooked smile.

"*Pike*, eh? She's no youngster," the chief said, spitting tobacco juice into a paper cup. "Been in service since the mid-thirties. You'll learn quick aboard her. Boats like that don't forgive mistakes."

Mason hesitated. "You've served on her?"

The chief shook his head. "Not *Pike*, no. But they're all the same. Steel, salt, and sweat. Treat her like she's alive, and maybe she'll keep you alive. Forget that, and..." He trailed off, leaving the rest unsaid.

Mason nodded, unsettled.

By the time they crossed into Ohio, Mason had fallen into the rhythm of travel. The flat plains stretched forever, endless fields dotted with barns and silos. They reminded him of home, and he thought of his father bent over the soil, his hands rough with work. Mason had left that behind, trading dirt and crops for steel and sea. He wondered if he'd ever see those fields again.

At night he lay awake in his berth, staring at the dark ceiling of the train car. He listened to the wheels clacking, the snores of fellow passengers, the occasional wail of a whistle as they thundered through sleeping towns. He felt both terribly small and terribly large, small in the vast country, large in the knowledge that he was part of something greater.

West of Denver the land rose in jagged peaks. The Rockies loomed, snow already dusting their tops. The train wound higher and higher, through tunnels and along cliffs where the ground dropped away in dizzying gulfs. Mason leaned out the window to breathe the thin, cold air, his heart pounding with wonder.

The mountains gave way at last to deserts, endless stretches of sand and scrub, red mesas burning under the sun. The heat pressed into the cars, dry and relentless. At small towns the train stopped for water, and Mason saw sunburned men in wide hats working the rails, children chasing stray dogs in dusty streets.

He bought a newspaper at one stop. The headlines spoke of politics in Europe, of unrest in Asia, of storms battering the Midwest. The world seemed wide and dangerous, and Mason felt himself being drawn into its currents.

Days later, the Pacific came into view. The smell of salt filled the air, sharper than the river tang of Connecticut. The train curved along the coast, gulls wheeled overhead, and the horizon stretched blue and endless. Mason's pulse quickened. He was almost there.

The Navy base at San Diego was alive with noise and motion. Destroyers and cruisers lined the piers, their masts bristling with antennae. Men hurried in every direction, carrying crates, coiling lines, barking orders. The air smelled of paint, hot steel, and the unmistakable tang of fuel oil.

Mason paused with his seabag slung over his shoulder and took it all in. This was the Pacific Fleet, the other edge of America, the frontier where the ocean stretched wide and empty.

"Submariner?" a petty officer asked, noticing the orders in his hand.

"Yes, sir. *Pike*," Mason said.

The man jerked his chin toward the harbor. "You'll want the *Holland*. She's anchored out there."

Mason followed his gaze. Out in the bay, a large tender floated at anchor, cranes jutting from her deck like arms. Boats swarmed around her, launches ferrying men and supplies back and forth. Steam curled from her funnels, and she bristled with activity.

The petty officer grinned. "Mother hen to the lot of you. *Holland* keeps your kind running."

Mason squinted. Alongside the tender lay a low, dark shape barely breaking the surface. From this distance it seemed unimpressive, like a whale resting against its mother. But he knew at once, that was *Pike*.

He waited for a launch, clutching his seabag as he climbed aboard. The boat rocked gently, spray cool on his face as they motored across the harbor. Closer now, *Holland* loomed like a floating factory. Her paint was weathered, her cranes busy, cables and hoses snaking down into the waiting submarine.

And there she was. *Pike*.

She looked smaller than Mason had imagined. Her deck barely cleared the water, her conning tower squat and plain. The paint on her hull was streaked with rust, her lines more workmanlike than sleek. She wasn't the poster-boat he had dreamed of, she was scarred, tired, alive.

Mason's chest tightened. This was his boat.

He shifted his seabag and stared, memorizing every detail: the narrow deck, the sailors moving easily over it, the soft rumble that seemed to come from her steel skin.

He thought again of his instructors' warnings: *"The boat is a living thing. Respect her, or she'll kill you."*

The launch bumped gently against *Holland*'s side. Mason rose, heart hammering, and prepared to climb. Soon he would cross the tender's deck, descend into *Pike*, and begin the real work of becoming a submariner.

He drew a deep breath, the smell of oil and salt filling his lungs. Sub School had given him books and drills. *Pike* would give him truth.

As the sun dipped toward the horizon, casting the harbor in gold, Mason felt the weight of his orders in his pocket and the greater weight of the life before him.

For the first time, he understood: his real schooling was about to begin.

Chapter 2
The Gauntlet

The launch came in crooked on the swell, thumping against the tender's gray flank with a hollow boom that Mason felt in his knees. Spray flashed and then fell away in glittering beads. The coxswain barked, "Boat secure!" and the two deckhands in dungarees threw their lines up to the waiting men on the tender. A rope ladder and a short, steep flight of metal steps hung down the ship's side like a tongue.

Mason gripped his seabag in his left hand and the rail with his right. From this close, the tender was a cliff, steel plates streaked with old paint, rivets like knuckles, scuppers breathing out a warm smell of steam and oil. She loomed so high and so near that he couldn't see her deck, only the edge where faces leaned over, watching the launch bob.

"Next man!" the coxswain snapped.

Mason stepped to the bottom of the steps, put the canvas bag on his shoulder, and started up. The first foot met a wet rung, and for a heartbeat he thought he'd slip backward into the froth. He locked his hand harder around the cold pipe, breathed through his nose, and climbed. The steps were too steep to be called a ladder and too straight to be called stairs. He hauled the bag, leg over leg, the soles of his shoes squealing on painted metal. When he popped up over the edge to the quarterdeck, the wind caught his hat brim and tried to take it. He jammed it back down with his elbow, reddening as two sailors smirked.

"Eyes front, sailor," one of them said, not unkindly. "Don't feed the gulls with your cover."

"Yessir," Mason said automatically, and immediately realized the man carried no officer's stripe, just a boatswain's mate crow on his sleeve. The smirk widened by a notch. It was the kind men wore when they smelled brand-new.

The plank trembled under his boots as he crossed to the tender. Engines throbbed somewhere deep inside, their vibration climbing through the soles of his shoes until it reached his chest. Men moved everywhere, voices sharp, boots clanging, lines creaking through wet pulleys. He had never seen so much gray steel in one place. It wasn't just a ship; it was an entire floating city that smelled of diesel and sweat and hot paint.

A gust of wind brought the taste of salt and oil. Mason's stomach turned, part fear, part excitement. Back home the world had been open fields and quiet dawns; here everything was enclosed, loud, alive. He touched the bulkhead as he passed, expecting cold metal but feeling warmth, as though the ship itself radiated a pulse. Someone shouted for him to keep moving. He did, swallowing hard, the clatter of the gangway echoing like a drumbeat marking the end of his old life.

The quarterdeck was a rectangle of clean paint and clean lines in the midst of hectic motion. A bright flag cracked at the stern. Somewhere forward a winch clattered. On this square, however, there was order: a line-box, a bell, a phone, a table with a blotter, and a young officer with an OOD armband standing behind it like a shopkeeper guarding his scales. A coxswain with a pistol belt, sidearm slung, posture bored, stood off to one side under an awning, watching everything and nothing.

Mason remembered Groton. *Salute the ensign, then the officer of the deck, then request permission to come aboard.* He set the seabag down at his feet, faced aft, raised his hand, held it a beat, and then turned to the officer. His fingertips found the brim, the gesture sharp enough.

"Sir, Seaman Second Class Daniel Mason reporting, orders for USS *Pike*."

The OOD's eyes flicked to the bag, then to Mason's shoes, then to his face. They were gray eyes, amused but not friendly.

"You're on *Holland*'s quarterdeck, sailor, not *Pike*'s," he said. His voice was dry as dust. "Let's try again with the words we use here." He spoke as if to a man tugging at the wrong end of a line. "You will say, 'Request permission to come aboard.' Then you will step to one side, keep your meat out of the way, and wait until someone tells you where to go."

"Yes, sir. Request permission to, "

The OOD raised one finger. "And before any of that, you will remember to salute your colors properly. You did it, but you rushed it like you were swatting a fly. We are not swatting flies on my quarterdeck. We are in the Navy."

The boatswain's mate made a tiny, appreciative cough. The coxswain smiled with the corner of his mouth and looked up at the awning as if it were the sky.

Heat crept up Mason's neck. "Aye aye, sir." He turned again, facing the stern where the flag snapped like a live thing. He raised his hand slowly, held it a clear second, lowered it with just as much care. Then he faced the OOD.

"Seaman Second Class Mason, sir. Request permission to come aboard."

"Granted." The OOD's tone did not change. "Orders."

Mason took the stiff envelope from his inside pocket and slid it across the blotter. The OOD didn't open it, only read the typed name on the front and the destination stamped in purple. He tapped the corner against the table, considering.

"*Pike*." There might have been a shade of humor there. "You folks always bring your gear like pack mules. Don't drop it down my ladder, Mason."

"No, sir."

"Good." The OOD lifted his chin toward the portside rail. "Subs are berthed portside, one deck below. You go straight down those stairs, then outboard over the brows. *Pike*'s three boats out. You will not, under any circumstance, go wandering around my decks with your mouth open like a cod. You will not light anything that smells like smoke. You will not put your big bag where a man can break his neck on it."

"Yes, sir."

"And one more thing." The OOD's eyes tracked to the seabag, then back to Mason. "You're a boat sailor now, at least you think you are. You're not on a boat yet. You will conduct yourself accordingly on *Holland*. You'll ask, not assume. If you don't know how to do a thing, you will ask. Do I make myself clear, Seaman Mason?"

"Clear, sir."

"Outstanding." The OOD slid the envelope back without comment. "Portside. Down one deck. If you fall off my stairs, I'll have you mopped up before evening chow."

"Aye aye." He shouldered the bag and pivoted. The boatswain's mate stepped neatly aside, not quite masking his grin.

"Welcome to the Fleet," the bosun murmured as Mason passed. "And eyes open on those stairs. They bite."

The tender's deck beyond the quarterdeck line was a city street at rush hour. Men in dungarees hauled hoses fat as a man's thigh toward waiting reels. A crane squealed and swung, lowering a pallet of crates to a hatch where hands reached up like ants. Steam ghosted from a vent and smelled of hot iron and coffee. Inboard, somewhere deep, something thumped rhythmically, part of the tender's heartbeat. Mason threaded his way along the painted path, hugging the rail not to be underfoot. Twice he had to stop and flatten himself to let a work party pass, each man carrying a length of pipe on one shoulder, their boots thudding in unison.

He reached the portside break where metal stairs dove steeply down against the hull. The outboard face of the ship fell away in a gray plane, and the stairs clung to it like a fire escape, narrow and uncompromising. Beyond the bottom landing, and just a little forward, he could see the low silhouettes of submarines riding on short lines, the first one pressed snug against the tender's skin, the next tied outboard of her, and the third beyond, low in the water, barely more than a smear of darker gray with a conning tower and a deck gun. Even before he looked for the stenciled name, he knew that outer shape had to be *Pike*: she sat a little lower, her paint streaked darker, her posture like an old dog lying with its head up, watchful.

"Hey." Mason turned. A lean deckhand with a wrench in his fist was watching him from beside a vent trunk, grease under his nails, eyes almost kind. "You part of that *Pike* draft?"

"Yes," Mason said. "Seaman Mason."

The man jerked his chin at the stairs. "Take it slow. Keep your bag high on your shoulder; it catches on the side otherwise. And when you hit the first brow, don't just hop across, even if you think nobody's looking. Boats get possessive. You ask. You ask loud enough they can hear you over the compressor, or they'll make sport of you. Got it?"

Mason felt gratitude surge up, unexpected and strong. "Got it. Thanks."

The deckhand shrugged. "Don't thank me. Just don't fall and knock your teeth out on my watch. Down you go."

The stairs were as steep as they looked, steeper. The wind that had snapped the flag held still down here, replaced by the wet breath of the harbor. The smell changed the way smells do when you step from a field into a machine shed: sudden, intimate. Oil and bilge, tar and paint, the raw, damp odor of ropes that had known a hundred tides. He took the first three steps cautiously and then found a rhythm, down, bag up and forward, down, knee not through the rung because the space was tight, down. The metal pinged under his heels. When he reached the small landing, it tilted slightly under his weight, a reminder that all this was afloat and obedient to the water's unthinking will.

The brow to the first submarine was a narrow bridge of steel with side chains, pitched just enough to remind a man he was between things, neither tender nor boat, neither safe nor in danger. Mason set his bag down at the tender's side long enough to face aft. The ensign was not visible here, hidden by the bulk of the tender, but old habits and brand-new instruction made him lift his hand anyway. He turned toward the submarine's deck. Two men stood by the forward hatch: one with a clip board, the other with a line coiled like a sleeping snake over his shoulder. Above them, beneath the conning tower's shield, a third man sat on a folding chair that had no business on a warship, his feet flat, forearms on thighs, a cigarette sheltering in the lee of his palm. The third man was the one who watched, the way a cat watches.

"Request permission to cross!" Mason called. His voice came out louder than he meant and then promptly vanished under a cough of air from some vent ahead. He tried again, pitching his voice like an instructor in Groton had taught them: from the belly, not the throat. "Request permission to cross!"

The man in the chair didn't move. The one with the line grinned.

"Permission, he says," the line-handler drawled without looking at the clipboard man. "Hear that? Permission. Will you listen to the manners on this one."

The clipboard man didn't smile. He had the expression of a schoolteacher who had been at it too long. "Where are your eyes, sailor?"

Mason blinked. "My eyes?"

"Flag, boy." The man tipped his head toward the short staff rigged on the submarine's after structure. On the tender's sheltered side, out of the wind, the boat had her little ensign up, bright and very close. *You might have seen it,* the man's face said coolly, *if you were not looking at your own shoes.* "We don't salute the tender's flag for us. We have our own."

Heat came again, quick and humiliating. Mason turned smartly and saluted the boat's colors, then came back to the brow and found the man in the folding chair finally watching him full-on. The older sailor took a last drag and ground the stub in a steel ashtray between his boots. His hat was low, shadowing his eyes.

"You've got a tongue," the man said. "Use it."

"Seaman Mason, orders to USS *Pike*. Request permission to cross your deck to reach my boat."

"That's better," the older man said, and it was almost approval. "Permission to cross granted." He jabbed a thumb toward the narrow bridge. "If you can do it without killing yourself. Watch the gap. The tender rides easy; we don't. And don't step on my telephone line. You'll know it if you do, because you'll hear me all day in your nightmares."

Mason swallowed, hefted the bag, and put his first foot on the brow. The metal clanked and shifted. He moved anyway, eyes flicking down to the outboard edge where a thick black cable ran along the plating and over the brow in a smooth hump. He stepped wide, over it, grateful for the warning. Up close the submarine felt alive in a way the tender hadn't, subtle motions, a low hum somewhere beneath his feet, the sense of something brooding that was not the sea. He crossed, reached the deck, and paused on the narrow plating, unsure where to put his bag.

"Not there," the line-handler said dryly as Mason hovered near a cleat. "Unless you want to see it go to the bottom. Hug the tower and keep moving, hero."

"Thanks," Mason murmured, and moved.

Between the first boat and the second there was only a few feet of water, a black seam where fenders squeaked and dripped. The second submarine lay outboard with her own small noises: the hiss of air down a hose, the growl of a pump, the slap of a hand against a hull in rhythm with some unseen chore. Her crew seemed fewer on deck, only one man at the hatch, cap pushed back, jaw working on a wad of something. Chewing tobacco, maybe. He watched Mason approach without interest.

"Request permission to cross," Mason said, not as loud as before but steady. He saluted the little flag mounted aft that he'd learned to look for first. The man at the hatch didn't even pivot.

"Cross," he said, tapping ash off the end of a cigarette he'd palmed somewhere. "Just don't knock your brains out on the shears. We just got the damn periscope greased."

Mason moved, grateful and slightly off-balance at the lack of ceremony. The brow dipped under his weight and rose again. His bag tried to pull him sideways; he corrected without thinking. The deck plates were slick with a thin skin of salt; his heels whispered on them. Outboard, the third boat lay low and a little sullen, as if she would have preferred to be alone. *Pike.*

He stopped at the outer brow. There was no one sitting in a folding chair here. No one smoking. No one grinning. The officer of the deck on *Pike* stood instead at the forward edge of the conning tower, one hand on the coaming, the other tucked under his elbow. He wore a peacoat open at the throat despite the sun. The coat made him look broader than he probably was. His hat sat square and low. Two men worked on deck aft of him, moving a hose by inches as if it were an anaconda with a temper.

Mason faced aft and saluted the small ensign mounted near the stern. The snap of it sounded wetter here, closer to the bay's breathing. He turned toward the conning tower and made himself take a breath before he spoke, the way the chief on the train had told him, though the chief had not meant lungs and words; he'd meant *think first, boy.*

"Seaman Second Class Mason," he called, and his voice carried well. "Orders to USS *Pike.* Request permission to come aboard."

The OOD didn't answer immediately. He watched Mason

with the unblinking attention of a man reading a gauge that mattered. Then he nodded. Not much. Just enough.

"Permission granted," he said. His voice had none of the tender's dryness, none of the first boat's sneer, none of the second boat's boredom. It had a different quality altogether, flat, controlled, a voice that might be at home in a dark room with the lights out and the pressure rising. "Cross carefully. Mind your bag. You drop it, you swim for it, because I'm not giving you a second one."

"Aye aye." Mason lifted the bag and set his shoe on the brow.

The metal shifted, not badly, but enough that his instincts woke fully. He felt his calf muscles tighten, his grip on the rope handline find its comfort, his center move just a hair inboard so that if the brow bounced he'd be with it and not against it. He was conscious of his hat, which the wind might still try to take, of his sleeve, which might catch on a split ring if he got too close, of the petty humiliations he'd already piled up and how easily more could accumulate. He found himself breathing deep to clear the harbor smell and the tender tang and simply take the salt as it was.

He stepped to the submarine's deck. It felt narrower than the first two, a little lower, a little less forgiving. The paint near the brow's landing was worn to a polish; a thousand men before him had come and gone here, and their footsteps had told the steel something about human persistence. He drew himself up because the OOD was watching and because, suddenly, the idea of slouching on this deck felt like slouching in front of an altar.

He had to say the words again, he knew that much. The ritual mattered. Face aft, salute the flag, face the watch, ask permission to come aboard. But his hands had begun to sweat despite the cool, and the bag's strap had begun to bite into the muscle above his shoulder blade.

He set the bag down by his left boot, neat to the conning tower's shadow where it would not be under a man's stride or a hose's path. He squared his cover and filled his lungs, readying the words he'd practiced out loud in the train car and under his breath on the pier, the words men had spoken on decks from Portsmouth to Manila.

"Hold."

The OOD's interruption was not sharp, only perfectly placed, precisely at the moment before Mason's mouth opened. The officer had stepped down from the tower as quietly as a tall man can descend a ladder. Up close he looked younger than the voice suggested, the hard edge of experience running across features that were still fine around the eyes. He wore no weapon, no ornament. Only the armband at his sleeve and the watchfulness in him marked him as the quarterdeck's authority.

"Before you give me your speech," the OOD said, "do you know why you're saying it?"

Mason blinked. He could feel the two deckhands behind the officer pause in their work, not turning but listening because you always listened when the man with the duty stopped to speak. "Sir?"

The OOD's mouth twitched, not quite a smile. "Not to me, Mason. You'll say it to the boat. You'll say it because she's not the tender and she's not the pier. She's a world, and she has rules. The words help you remember you're crossing into them."

"Yes, sir," Mason said, and it felt different to say it here, with the steel under his soles and the water shouldering at the hull.

"Good." The OOD tipped his head aft. "Proceed."

Mason faced the stern and raised his hand. The flag snapped. He held the salute a heartbeat longer than he had on the tender's quarterdeck, not to please the officer but because the pause felt correct. He lowered his hand, turned back to the OOD, squared his shoulders until the seabag strap bit in a friendly way, and let the words come, clear and measured.

"Seaman Second Class Daniel Mason, reporting for duty by orders to USS *Pike*, sir. Request permission to come aboard."

The OOD's eyes did not leave his face. For a fraction of a second nothing moved, only the gentle seesaw of the deck, the small hiss of the hose aft, the far-off clank of the tender's crane.

And then the officer nodded once, an exact echo of the nod he had given from the tower, and opened his mouth to answer.

The OOD's nod was all the permission Mason needed, but before he could move, the forward hatch clanged. A pair of hands gripped the coaming and a head appeared, followed by broad shoulders in a sweat-darkened chambray shirt.

"New man, eh?" The voice carried up before the rest of him did. The sailor hauled himself out of the hole with the ease of long practice, ducked under the railing, and gave Mason a long, slow once-over. He was older, maybe thirty, but weather had written him into harder lines than his years. His forearms were roped with muscle, his hair cropped close, and his eyes quick and measuring.

The OOD's mouth twitched into something like relief. "Nolan. Just in time. Take this one below before he gets run over."

"Aye, sir." Nolan wiped his palms on his trouser thighs, then stuck out a hand. "Name's Nolan. You're Mason, I take it?"

"Yes, sir, uh, I mean, aye." Mason grabbed the hand. Nolan's grip was iron, brief but certain.

"Don't 'sir' me, kid. Save that for officers. I work for a living." He released Mason's hand and pointed to the seabag. "That yours?"

"Yes, Petty Officer."

"Then get it squared up. And mind your head, mind your hands, and don't ever put yourself where the boat can chew you." Nolan slung the bag one-handed as if it weighed nothing and jerked his chin toward the hatch. "Follow me."

The hatch yawned black and narrow. Mason leaned over, peering into it. A steep ladder plunged into dimness, rungs glistening with oil and sweat. The smell rolled up at him, diesel, metal, and the unmistakable scent of men packed close. It was sharp, heavy, not like the crisp tang of the harbor. This was something else, something intimate and lived-in.

"Down you go," Nolan said. "Feet first. Always feet first." He slung Mason's bag ahead of him, letting it slide down into waiting hands below. "Use both hands. And if you're stupid enough to miss, you'll wish you'd never been born."

Mason swallowed. He gripped the sides and swung his legs into the hole. The steel was cold under his palms. The ladder rattled as he set his boots on the first rung, then the second. He felt the hatch ring scrape his shoulders as he squeezed through. Then the world narrowed.

Light slanted weakly from shaded bulbs. He counted the rungs, every clang of his soles echoing into the compartment. The air was hotter down here, close enough that he felt sweat prick under his uniform even before his boots touched deck.

"Step off, kid," a voice said.

Mason looked down to see two sailors steadying his bag. He hopped the last step, landing on a steel deck that seemed too narrow to deserve the name. Pipes crawled the overhead like veins. Wires snaked in bundles. Every inch of space was claimed by something, valves, gauges, lockers, ladders, men.

Nolan followed, swinging down with no need for rungs, boots slapping as if the boat were part of him. He pointed Mason aft.

"Forward torpedo room," Nolan said. "Where you're standing now. Mind the deck. Torpedoes ride here. Don't trip a lanyard or you'll learn about explosives quick."

Mason looked around. The room was long, crowded, and dominated by the massive cylinders of torpedo tubes. A faint tang of grease and metal shavings hung in the air. Sailors in undershirts moved around them, tools clanking, voices muttering in the narrow space. Every man seemed to know exactly where to put his feet, how to turn his shoulders. Mason felt like a plow horse dropped into a dance hall.

One of the sailors grinned when he saw Mason's uncertain look. "Fresh fish," he said loudly. "Smell's still on him."

The others laughed. Mason flushed.

"Enough," Nolan said, his tone flat but with weight. The laughter died immediately. "He's mine. I'll square him away."

Nolan started aft at a steady pace, Mason hurrying to keep up. The deck was narrow, bunks stacked three high to one side, each with a curtain and a bit of personal clutter. The smell of sweat and old socks was strong. The overhead was low; Mason ducked instinctively, but still knocked his hat brim on a pipe.

"First lesson," Nolan said without slowing. "You'll bleed from the head until you learn to duck without thinking. Second lesson, you'll learn where to plant your feet so you don't end up on your ass every time the boat rolls. Third lesson, if you don't know what a valve does, you don't touch it. Not for fun, not for curiosity, not even if it looks like it needs turning."

"Yes, Petty Officer." Mason tried to keep his voice steady, though it was hard with the boat pressing in from every side.

Nolan glanced back at him. "You'll call me Nolan or Chief, not Petty Officer. We're not polishing language in here, we're keeping a boat alive."

"Yes, Chief."

"That's better."

They passed into the control room. It was the heart of the boat, a cramped space crammed with dials, wheels, and levers. The periscope well rose like a tree trunk through the deck, polished from a hundred hands. A helmsman leaned casually on the wheel, one foot braced, chatting with another sailor. They barely glanced at Mason, though he felt their eyes after he passed.

Nolan pointed as they walked. "Here's where the magic happens. Planes, rudder, ballast controls. Everything that keeps us from being a steel coffin. Learn it well enough and you'll live. Screw it up and you'll kill twenty-five men before you drown yourself."

Mason's mouth was dry. He nodded.

Aft again, the air turned hotter, more sour. The engine room roared with a muted thunder, two big diesels throbbing like angry beasts. Men shouted over the din, sweat streaking their faces. The smell of fuel oil was thick enough to taste. Mason's stomach lurched.

"Engines," Nolan said, raising his voice. "The boys back here are loud and mean. You'll get used to it. If you don't, the smell will toughen you until nothing ever bothers you again."

Mason could barely hear him, but he nodded anyway.

Past the engines lay the after torpedo room, smaller, tighter, but no less crowded. Torpedoes gleamed in their racks, their warheads painted dull green. Two men lay on bunks directly over them, reading magazines as if they were resting above barrels of apples.

Nolan stopped and finally set Mason's bag down. "That's the grand tour. Forward fish, after fish, everything in between. *Pike*'s a Porpoise-class, one of the first of the big fleet boats. She's not young, but she's got teeth if you treat her right. You treat her wrong..." He let the thought trail off, the weight of it heavier than any words.

Mason stared at the bag, at the torpedoes, at the boat pressing in around him. His heart thudded against his ribs.

Nolan clapped a hand on his shoulder, firm and steady. "You made it aboard. That's the hardest part for some. Now we make you useful."

Nolan led him back toward the control room. The passage seemed narrower now, though Mason was starting to move with more rhythm. He ducked automatically under one pipe and felt a flash of pride that it hadn't cracked him.

"You'll be mess-cooking first," Nolan said. "Scrub pans, fetch coffee, haul trash. Don't think you're too good for it. Every man does his time. You'll learn faces, names, and who not to cross. You'll earn your keep until you're trusted with more."

"Yes, Chief."

"And while you're hauling garbage, you'll watch. Every valve, every gauge, every wheel. You'll ask questions when you can. You'll make yourself useful. That's how you get your dolphins. Understand?"

"Yes, Chief."

Nolan gave him another measuring look. "You'll do." He stopped near the ladder that led back to the forward hatch. "Get your gear stowed. I'll have someone show you your rack. Then you'll report to the mess cook. And Mason?"

"Yes, Chief?"

Nolan's mouth quirked, not quite a smile but close.

"Welcome to *Pike*. She's a mean old girl, but if you learn to listen, she'll keep you alive."

Mason set his seabag down and let out a slow breath. The steel pressed close, the smells were overwhelming, and the boat felt like it was humming under his boots, as if she were alive, waiting to see what kind of man he was.

He thought back to Groton, to the instructors who had said the boat was more than steel. He hadn't believed it then. He wasn't sure he did now. But as Nolan's footsteps faded down the passage and the *Pike* shifted gently on her mooring, Mason couldn't shake the feeling that the submarine was listening.

And that his real trial had only just begun.

Chapter 3
Mess Cook & Greenhorn

The galley was hotter than hell and half the size.

Daniel Mason had imagined life on a submarine might mean working with gleaming machinery, or at least standing in the control room with his hand on a wheel. Instead, within a day of reporting aboard, he found himself wedged in a space the size of his family's chicken coop, arms elbow-deep in a steel pan coated with an inch of black grease.

"Scrub harder, mess cook."

The voice came from behind him, the *Pike*'s cook, a wiry first class with a sharp nose and permanent grease stains on his dungarees. His name was McCracken, but the crew called him Mac, and he carried himself like a man who had survived ten years of trying to make submariners eat food that barely deserved the name.

"Yes, Sir," Mason muttered, grinding the brush harder

against the stubborn crust. His hands were already raw from lye soap.

"Not 'sir,' not 'Chief,'" Mac said, leaning over to peer into the pot. "This is my kingdom. You're my slave. Understand?"

"Yes, Mac."

"Good boy." He shoved another pan onto the tiny steel counter. "Welcome to your new life."

Mason's world for the next week shrank to the mess deck. It wasn't a room so much as a passage that happened to have a stove crammed in one corner and a pair of folding tables bolted to the deck. Bunks were stacked right above the tables, so when the off-watch came to eat, they were climbing out of bed and sitting down in the same breath. The air was a stew of smells: diesel and sweat, cabbage boiling in the galley, the acrid bite of coffee burned on the hotplate, oilcloth, wet socks, and humanity. Mason gagged the first time he tried to eat in it.

"Get used to it," Mac said. "The boat smells like this when she's happy."

He wasn't sure what that meant, but in the days that followed he began to understand. The whole boat was alive, sweating, humming, breathing through the ducts. Every sound had a purpose. The rattle of the stove fan meant ventilation. The drip of a condensation line told him the air coolers were doing their job. When one of those sounds stopped, even for a heartbeat, the silence was worse than noise.

And he never seemed to stop moving.

"Coffee, messman!" someone barked.

"More chow up here!"

"Hey, new guy, you forgot the bread!"

Mason scrambled like a man on fire. He slopped coffee into mugs, fetched trays, peeled mountains of potatoes in the scullery. When he spilled a ladle of soup into a chief's lap, the whole compartment erupted in laughter.

"Watch yourself, mess cook!" the chief barked, standing to wipe his trousers. "You trying to scald me into early retirement?"

Mason stammered apologies, face crimson.

"Relax, kid," another sailor chuckled. "You're still new. You'll get it right eventually. Or you'll drown trying."

That set off another round of laughter, some good-natured, some not.

The only steady hand in the storm was Nolan. The chief petty officer seemed to appear whenever Mason was on the verge of breaking. He never coddled, never spared him the truth, but he had a way of anchoring Mason when the boat's chaos threatened to sweep him away.

One evening, Mason was scrubbing pans in the scullery, sweat dripping from his chin. Nolan leaned against the bulkhead, arms folded.

"You think you're scrubbing dishes," Nolan said. "But you're learning the boat."

Mason glanced up, bewildered. "Doesn't feel like it."

"Look around." Nolan pointed with his chin. "That pipe above your head, saltwater line. Runs forward to the ballast tanks. Hear the faint hiss? That's how you know it's flowing right. If it sounds wrong, you'll know she's sick. That breaker there, feeds the stove. Overload it and you'll black out half the mess deck. Every inch of this place has meaning. Learn it while you peel your potatoes, or you'll never catch up."

Mason straightened, listening harder. The hiss of the pipe, the faint vibration under his boots, he hadn't noticed them until Nolan pointed.

"I... I think I get it."

"You don't. Not yet. But you will." Nolan's mouth twitched. "Keep at it, Mason. The boat's talking all the time. Learn her language."

Nolan's advice took root. Mason started noticing things: the slow rise and fall of air pressure when the hatch above opened; the way deck plates clicked differently when the tanks were full. Even the hum of the generators seemed to change pitch depending on who was on watch. It was as if the *Pike* were whispering secrets, and only the attentive could hear.

Not everyone was inclined to help. Horvath, a machinist's mate with arms like railroad ties, seemed to take particular delight in tormenting Mason. He tripped him with a broom handle once, sending mugs flying. Another time he handed Mason a bucket of galley slop.

"Dump it over the side," Horvath said with a grin.

Mason had just reached the hatch when Nolan stopped him cold. "What the hell do you think you're doing?"

"Dumping it, he told me, "

"Subs don't heave garbage out like some tramp steamer. You'd have the whole boat stinking to high heaven. There's a procedure. Don't let them hang you out like that."

Nolan turned a glare on Horvath. "You think it's funny, making a fresh fish screw up? You do it again, you'll explain yourself to the COB."

Horvath scowled, muttering under his breath, but he backed down.

Later, Nolan told Mason quietly, "They'll test you. If you don't know, ask. Better to look green than look dead."

The days blurred together, endless coffee runs, endless pans, endless orders shouted down the passage. But Mason began to find rhythm.

He learned to wedge his hip against the table when the boat rolled, so the tray didn't slide. He learned the crew's quirks: Jensen liked his coffee black, Morales wanted sugar, Mac cursed in three languages when he burned bacon. He learned how to move through the boat like water, duck here, sidestep there, brace your knee before the lurch. The first time he walked the length of the mess deck without banging his head on the infamous low pipe, he felt like a king.

There were quiet moments too. After midnight, when the boat was still and most of the crew slept, Mason would sit on the galley stool, listening. The hum of the fans. The heartbeat throb of a pump somewhere deep. Sometimes he imagined he could feel the *Pike* breathing, slow, steady, protective. Other times, when she groaned in the swells, she sounded almost angry, like a beast straining at its leash.

One night, after brewing a pot of coffee so strong it made even Horvath grunt, "Not bad, messman," Mason lay in his bunk with a quiet smile. It wasn't much, but it was something. He'd survived his first week without spilling soup on another chief, and he was starting to hear the boat's voice, faint, patient, alive.

Sleep came fitful in the narrow rack. But Mason found himself listening to the *Pike* in the dark. The faint thrum of pumps. The whisper of air cycling. The creak of steel as she shifted against her mooring. He realized he could tell when the diesels started up even before the vibration reached the deck. He could smell the change in the air when a vent was opened.

The instructors back at Groton had said the boat was a living thing. Mason had laughed at the idea. But now, in the dark, with steel pressing inches from his nose and the rhythm of machinery surrounding him, he wasn't so sure.

Maybe *Pike* really was alive. Maybe she was watching him, waiting to see if he was worth her time.

For now he was only the mess cook, scrubbing pans and spilling coffee. But he could feel it: sooner or later, the boat would demand more of him.

And when she did, he'd have to answer.

The chance came sooner than Mason expected. Two weeks into his sentence as galley slave, Mac finally took pity, or maybe just wanted him out of the way. "Kid," the cook said, wiping his hands on a rag that was darker than his dungarees, "you ever been aft?" Mason shook his head. "Good. Go down there and tell Chief Nolan I need that breaker checked before I burn this damn stove out. And don't touch anything unless he tells you to."

The after passageway felt different from the mess deck, tighter, hotter, the air dense with oil and machine sweat. As he ducked through the hatch, the sound changed too: not the clatter of pans or the hiss of steam, but a deep, rhythmic growl that seemed to vibrate in his ribs. The *Pike*'s heart was beating down here.

"Permission to enter, Chief?" he called over the noise.

Nolan looked up from a crouch beside the port diesel, his face streaked with grease. "You can come in, Mason. Keep your head down unless you like the taste of steel."

He pointed to a bank of gauges. "Breaker panel's back there. You ever seen one before?"

"Only in school, sir."

"Don't call me sir," Nolan said with a grin. "I work for a living."

Mason knelt beside him, watching the Chief's hands move with a surgeon's steadiness, checking connections, tapping gauges, feeling heat by instinct. The engines thundered, and yet Nolan seemed to hear something underneath them, something subtle and alive.

"She talks to us," Nolan said, almost shouting over the noise. "Every pump, every bearing, every valve's got a voice. Once you learn her song, you'll know when she's off-key." Mason listened. The engines didn't just make noise, they had rhythm: the steady thump of pistons, the whisper of air through vents, the flutter when a fuel injector missed by half a beat. He found himself nodding unconsciously, feeling it rather than hearing it.

"Good," Nolan said, catching the motion. "You've got the ear for it. That's rare."

For the next hour Mason watched, fetched tools, and tried not to get in the way. The deck plates quivered under his boots, the air thick with diesel exhaust. Sweat ran down his back, but for the first time aboard *Pike*, he didn't feel out of place. The machinery made sense to him, each valve, each pulse of vibration fitting together like the gears of a clock.

When they finally shut the engines down and the compartment fell into humming silence, Nolan handed him a rag. "You did all right. Stick around a few more watches. The galley can spare you once in a while."

From then on, whenever he wasn't peeling potatoes, Mason found excuses to drift aft. He learned the order of startup, air blowers, lube pumps, ignition sequence. He memorized the smell of hot oil when the bearings ran too dry, the slight pitch change when a clutch engaged. The men began to tolerate him. Horvath even stopped sneering long enough to explain the fuel manifold, though he still called him "mess cook" with a grin.

The first time Nolan let him take readings alone, Mason nearly burst with pride. The logbook was sacred; touching it meant trust. He moved carefully down the line, pencil trembling in one hand, flashlight in the other. The numbers meant more than figures, they were proof the boat was alive and well.

Later, when the engines were secured and the *Pike* shifted to battery, he lingered by the aft bulkhead. The silence felt deeper than before, almost holy. He laid a hand on the warm steel.

"You did good tonight," he whispered, unsure whether he meant the machinery or himself.

The metal seemed to hum beneath his palm, answering in its own language.

That night he couldn't sleep. The rhythm of the engines still echoed in his bones, a phantom throb like a heartbeat. He understood, finally, what Nolan had meant, the boat wasn't just a machine. She was a creature, breathing through pipes, dreaming through wires, trusting her men to keep her alive.

When Mason woke for morning mess, the thought stayed with him. He moved differently through the passageway now, ducking instinctively under pipes, balancing with the boat's motion as though they shared the same pulse. Even Mac noticed. You look like you finally got your sea legs," the cook said. "Maybe I did," Mason replied. "Maybe the boat gave 'em to me."

Mac squinted, then snorted. "Careful, kid. Start talking like that and they'll think you're going soft in the head."

But Mason only smiled. He knew better now. The *Pike* wasn't just steel and rivets. She was something more, something alive, and she'd just decided to let him belong.

The next morning, Mason was summoned to the crew's mess with a summons he didn't expect. Chief Nolan stood by the hatch with a clipboard under his arm and that same measured half-smile that never reached his eyes.

"Messman Mason," Nolan said. "The galley says they can survive without you for a while. Congratulations, you're moving aft."

Mason blinked. "Engine room, Chief?"

"Don't sound so surprised. You've been sniffing around there every chance you get. Figured it's time to see if you can tell a lube pump from your elbow."

The words hit like liberty after a long watch. Mason stammered out a "Thank you, Chief," but Nolan cut him short with a raised hand.

"Don't thank me yet. You screw this up, and Mac will have you peeling potatoes until the next war."

The after compartments felt like another world. The heat came from the engines now, not the galley stove, and the air carried the metallic tang of oil and ozone. Nolan walked him through the narrow space, pointing with the tip of his wrench.

"This," he said, tapping a thick pipe, "is your life. Saltwater line. Don't open it unless you enjoy high-pressure showers. Over here, main lube oil sump. Smell that? That's what keeps the bearings singing instead of screaming."

Mason followed every motion, notebook in hand, sketching rough diagrams that ended up streaked with grease. For hours he traced lines by touch, learning valves by feel when he couldn't see them. The boat throbbed faintly around him, steady and alive.

When they took a break, Nolan handed him a tin cup of coffee black enough to stand a spoon. "You're catching on," the Chief said. "Most new guys stare at gauges. You listen. That's better. Gauges lie, the boat doesn't."

That night, Mason was assigned his first engine-room watch. He stood beside the thundering Fairbanks-Morse diesels, eyes on the panel, ears tuned to every subtle shift. The Chief didn't hover, just nodded once in approval before disappearing forward. Alone with the machines, Mason felt something stir, recognition, maybe even communion. He could sense when a cylinder lagged, when a valve clattered just a hair too long. The vibrations told him what the instruments hadn't yet registered.

When Nolan returned, Mason hesitated before reporting. "Chief... number three sounds off. Half a beat slow."

The Chief listened, eyes narrowing. "Damn. Good catch." He adjusted a fuel lever, and the rhythm steadied. "Not bad for a mess cook."

For the rest of the watch, Nolan said little. But when the shift ended, he clapped Mason on the shoulder. "You've got a feel for her, kid. Don't lose it. The *Pike* only talks to those who listen."

Over the next weeks, Mason's days became a blur of watches, tracing out systems, and system diagrams. He learned to crawl through bilges to follow pipes from stem to stern, marking each with chalk. His hands were perpetually scraped; his fingernails never came clean again. Yet for all the exhaustion, he felt alive in a way he'd never known on land. The *Pike* was teaching him, and the lessons came in steel, sweat, and sound.

Sometimes, when the men slept and the diesels were secured, he'd linger in the quiet engine room. The residual warmth pulsed through the deck plates. He would rest his palm on the manifold and whisper, "Still with us, girl?" The faint tick of cooling metal answered him like a heartbeat.

Word spread that Mason was "making quals" faster than anyone expected. Even Horvath, grudgingly impressed, stopped his pranks. Mac sent down fresh coffee one night with a note scrawled on the side of the pot: *Don't let my best mess cook forget where he came from.*

But Mason hardly noticed the teasing anymore. He had joined the living rhythm of the boat, the synchronized ballet of air, oil, and motion. He moved through hatches with confidence, timing each step to the *Pike*'s subtle sway. Every clang, every hiss, every whisper of machinery wove itself into a single pulse that filled his veins.

One evening, as they ran drills off San Diego, the *Pike* rolled hard in a swell. A steam line vibrated loose, venting scalding mist into the compartment. Mason reacted without thinking, wrenching the valve shut and sealing the leak before the alarm even sounded. The Chief's voice barked from across the room.

"Who the hell caught that?"

"Mason, Chief."

Nolan stared for a beat, then nodded once. "Good instincts. You just saved us a flooded bilge, maybe worse."

Mason's hands shook after, but the pride burned steady beneath the adrenaline. That night, he couldn't sleep. The *Pike*'s breathing filled his dreams.

He was part of her now, not just crew, but pulse and sinew, one heartbeat among many. And though he didn't know it yet, the rhythm he'd learned in those narrow steel passages would one day carry him through fire, depth, and war.

Chapter 4
Outbound

The order came just before dawn: *Pike* was getting underway.

Mason had slept little, nerves keeping him half awake in his bunk. Every creak of the boat, every muffled voice outside his curtain, seemed to whisper that something was coming. When Nolan's hand shook his shoulder, Mason rolled out stiff and clammy.

"Up, mess cook," Nolan said. "Today's the day you learn if you've got sea legs."

Mason rubbed his eyes. "We're going out?"

"Sharp kid," Nolan said dryly. "Get your gear stowed tight. Anything loose becomes a missile once we hit the swells."

The mess deck buzzed louder than Mason had ever heard it. Men shouted, boots thumped, valves hissed. *Pike*'s hull seemed to come alive beneath him. He helped clear the mess tables, locking pans and mugs into racks, lashing down whatever might rattle.

Above, the sound of lines being heaved and cleats being hammered echoed down through the steel. A boatswain's whistle shrilled, followed by a call Mason couldn't quite make out. Then came the deep, resonant vibration, the diesels kicking over. The whole boat trembled as if she had shivered herself awake.

Mason felt it in his chest, a rhythm deeper than his own heartbeat.

"Diesels are up," Nolan said. "We'll be moving in minutes. You'd better get topside if you want to breathe fresh air before the fun starts."

Mason hesitated. "I thought I wasn't supposed to, "

Nolan waved him off. "Quarterdeck watch'll bark, but you're crew now. Go get a look. First time's always something."

Mason climbed the ladder and emerged onto *Pike*'s deck. The sky was just beginning to glow pink over San Diego. The tender *Holland* loomed astern, cranes folded, hoses coiled. Sailors on her rail gave half-interested waves as *Pike*'s lines were cast off.

The harbor stretched wide and calm. Destroyers and cruisers swung at anchor. The smell of tar and salt hung in the morning chill.

Pike's little deck trembled under Mason's boots as her

screws churned. Slowly, ponderously, she eased away from *Holland*'s side and into the channel.

The OOD glanced at Mason but said nothing, only jerked a thumb aft: stay out of the way. Mason obeyed, gripping the rail, trying to look like he belonged.

For a moment, as the sun broke over the horizon and painted the water gold, he felt pride surge in his chest. He was at sea. A submariner, outbound on patrol.

Then the swell hit.

It started as a queasy roll in his stomach, a little flutter that Mason thought he could master. But the swells outside the breakwater were heavier than he expected, long gray shoulders lifting *Pike* up and then dropping her down with a shudder.

Mason swallowed hard. His hands clenched the rail.

Nolan's voice came from behind him. "You're looking a little green, Mason."

"I'm fine," Mason said through clenched teeth.

"Sure you are." Nolan clapped him on the back. "Don't worry. Happens to everyone. Just don't puke on the deck. Puke over the side like a proper sailor."

Mason made it another ten minutes before his stomach betrayed him. He lurched to the side, leaned over the rail, and lost his breakfast in a long, miserable heave. Salt spray stung his face.

The laughter came immediately.

"Fresh fish over the side!" someone hollered.

"Better get used to it, kid!" another voice added.

Mason wiped his mouth, humiliated, and forced himself to stay upright. The boat rolled again, threatening to upend him, but he clung to the rail and swore he wouldn't let go.

Nolan only said, "Better out than in. Now get back below before the OOD throws you off his deck."

The air was worse inside. Hotter, thicker, infused with fuel oil and sweat. The steady vibration of the diesels made the bulkheads hum. The mess deck seemed even smaller now, with every man pressed shoulder to shoulder.

Mason staggered through the passageway, trying not to bump into anyone. The boat's roll made the deck shift under his boots. He spilled half a cup of coffee trying to carry it forward and earned a curse from a chief.

"Steady, messman!" the chief barked. "This ain't no barn dance!"

Mason mumbled an apology, cheeks burning.

The alarm hit without warning.

Klaxon horns wailed, a rising, urgent bray that made Mason's hair stand on end. Men shouted, boots pounded, hatches clanged.

"Crash dive! Crash dive!"

Mason froze in the mess deck, heart hammering. Nolan appeared like a ghost, seizing his shoulder.

"Move, damn you! Get out of the passage!" Nolan shoved him against the bulkhead as men thundered past, scrambling to their stations. The deck canted sharply as *Pike* angled down, her bow biting into the sea.

Mason felt his stomach lurch as the boat tilted. He grabbed a pipe to steady himself. Water hissed somewhere forward, the ballast tanks flooding. The diesels roared higher, then cut abruptly. The sudden silence was deafening, replaced a moment later by the shriek of blowers and the whine of motors.

Lights flickered.

"Depth fifty feet!" someone shouted.

The deck tilted more. Mason slid half a step before Nolan's hand steadied him. Men moved like parts of a machine, voices clipped and precise. Mason could only cling to the bulkhead, wide-eyed.

"Leveling off at seventy-five," another voice reported.

The angle eased. The boat steadied, humming under the pull of her motors.

Nolan leaned close, voice steady despite the chaos. "That's a crash dive, Mason. You've got about thirty seconds to get below when you hear that klaxon, or the ocean takes you. Remember it."

Mason nodded dumbly, sweat running down his back.

The drill ended as abruptly as it began. The klaxon cut off. Voices relaxed, the tension bleeding away. Men wiped their brows, grinning, ribbing each other about seconds gained or lost.

Mason sagged against the bulkhead, legs shaking.

"You did fine," Nolan said.

"I froze."

"You didn't get killed. That's step one." Nolan clapped him on the shoulder. "Next time, you'll move faster. That's how it works."

Mason swallowed. "How many next times are there?"

Nolan's eyes met his, calm but hard. "Until it's not a drill."

That night, Mason lay in his rack, stomach still queasy, ears ringing with the memory of the klaxon. Every creak of the boat, every faint groan of steel, reminded him how fragile this world was.

But he also remembered the moment *Pike* had leveled off, humming steady, alive under his boots. She hadn't failed. The crew hadn't failed.

Maybe he could belong here after all.

The sea didn't grow gentler overnight. It only learned new ways to lift and drop them.

By morning the long Pacific swell had a cross-chop on top of it, a second rhythm that made *Pike*'s motion unpredictable. Men moved with knees bent and one hand free. Mason learned why: the boat would lull, then heave without warning, and anything not tied down tried to go airborne.

"Runner!" the chief of the boat bellowed from the control room hatch. "Nolan, I want that fresh fish earning blisters!"

"Aye, COB." Nolan crooked a finger at Mason, who was ferrying a tray of mugs along the mess table. "You're on my hip. When I say go, you go. When I stop, you stop. Do not, " he jabbed a finger into Mason's chest ", run into a valve wheel. It'll win."

Mason set the mugs down, swallowed, and fell in behind Nolan as the older petty officer flowed forward into the control room.

It was a cramped, humming nerve center. The planesmen's hands rested on their wheels, light and sure. The diving officer stood with a clipboard, pencil behind one ear, eyes tracking the depth gauge as if he could move the needle by will alone. The periscope well rose like a throat through the deck, its polished steel smeared by palms.

"Flooding drill in five," the diving officer said, not looking up. "Simulate forward bilge. Chief, you'll get your spray. Mr. Harrigan wants times."

Nolan's mouth tipped in what might once have been a smile. "He always wants times. He'll get them when we have them."

He turned to Mason. "You'll be my legs. I call, you carry. Words clear, repeat them back to the man I point at, come back for the next. Don't make a detour to die somewhere."

"Understood," Mason said, though his heart was beating fast. He could still feel the memory of yesterday's crash dive in his bones, the tilt, the rushing water sounds, the sudden silence when the diesels cut. He rubbed his palms on his dungarees.

The klaxon didn't wail this time. A sharp whistle blew, then the diving officer raised his voice. "Commence flooding drill. Forward bilge. Make it spray."

Somewhere forward, a valve squealed and a nozzle spat a sheet of seawater into the forward torpedo room. The noise had a wolfish sound. Men shouted. The control room changed in a breath from idle watchfulness to intent action. Nolan's hand sliced the air and Mason was moving.

"Message for forward: isolate the bilge, verify suction on number two pump," Nolan said. It came even, like a cadence, and Mason repeated it out loud as he ran, so the words didn't slide out of his head when the boat rolled.

He squeezed past a pair of men wrestling a hose, ducked under a pipe he'd already learned to fear, skidded into the forward room with his shoulder catching a bulkhead. The spray made the deck slick and glittered in the yellow light. Two torpedomen in rolled-up sleeves worked a valve wheel together, their boots planted wide.

"Message from control!" Mason shouted, putting his back to the spray. "Isolate the bilge, verify suction on number two pump!"

"Already isolating!" one torpedoman yelled back without looking. "Tell control number two pump's sluggish!"

Mason ran. Back through the narrowing that never seemed big enough for a man with shoulders. The boat lifted under him, then fell, and for a second his stomach was in his throat again. He got to control without falling and spit the words at Nolan.

"Number two's sluggish."

Nolan didn't curse; he didn't have to. "Tell engine room: put their ears on number two pump; if she wheezes, swap to number three. On the double."

Mason ran aft this time, heat rising with every step. The engine room was a sauna of noise and motion. The two great diesels slept now, their bulk looming in the half-light, but motors sang through the deckplates, and the reek of oil was thick enough to taste.

"Message from control!" Mason shouted into the ear of a machinist's mate in a sweat-darkened shirt. "Ears on number two pump, if she wheezes, swap to number three!"

The machinist didn't bother with words. He pressed two fingers to his temple, heard you, and turned away, cupping his hands around his mouth to bellow into the din. Three men slid along the catwalk as if they rode rails. One leaned close to a casing, listening with the bones of his face. Another tapped a gauge. The third made a chopping motion and they moved together to a second manifold, hands sure.

Back to control. "Engine room listening. Standing by to swap to number three if two wheezes."

"Good," the diving officer muttered. "Forward reports?"

"Sluggish pump. They're isolating," Nolan said, which was as much praise as he'd give. He slanted a look at Mason. "You breathing?"

"Yes, Chief," Mason said, though his lungs felt too small and the air too hot.

"Keep breathing. We're not done." Nolan nodded to the planesman. "What's our angle?"

"Down two degrees, steady," the planesman said, not taking his eyes off the bubble.

Nolan sent Mason again and again, forward for status, aft for a wrench, to the battery compartment to tell a man to stand clear of a hatch, back to the mess to yank two burners off because someone had decided now was a fine time to boil coffee. Each run was a test: duck, sidestep, plant a boot, push, don't get killed. Twice his sleeve caught on something; twice he remembered at the last instant to pull and roll his shoulder before he tore himself open on a split pin.

The spray cut off. "Forward reports flooding secured," Mason panted to Nolan when he found breath.

"Time?" the diving officer snapped.

"Two minutes, twelve," a yeoman answered, pencil scratching furiously.

"Better," the diving officer said. "Still sloppy on the pump call. Again after lunch."

A low groan of good-natured complaint rose and fell like a wave. Nolan didn't bother to groan. He folded his arms and leaned one shoulder against the periscope well, eyes scanning faces the way a man counts tools.

He gave Mason a small nod. "You didn't die."

"I... tried not to," Mason said, which earned him three inches of Nolan's grin.

"Good policy."

They ran the drill twice more before noon, and the second time Mason didn't miss the step at the ladder, and the third time he slid past Horvath with a message and didn't flinch when the big machinist tried to shoulder him into a bulkhead. Nolan didn't say a word about that, but as Mason brushed past, he felt the briefest brush of the older man's knuckles against his elbow. It steadied him more than a speech.

After chow, beans that tasted like the inside of a locker and bread thick as deck planking, the diving officer called for electrical grounds testing. The electricians swarmed like bees. Mason hovered at the edge until Nolan jerked his chin toward a breaker panel. "Watch and listen. Don't touch."

The lead electrician, a narrow man with meticulous hands and a jaw that clenched when anyone breathed too loud, popped a panel and began to call numbers. His striker read them back. The words ran together like a prayer:

"Ground check good on number five bus… resistance steady… next."

Mason followed their eyes to the meter needle, watched it tremble and settle, tremble and settle. He realized the man's left hand was on the metal in the same way the engine room man had put his face to the pump casing. Listening, but with skin.

"Why the two hands?" Mason murmured to Nolan.

"Redundancy," Nolan murmured back. "Eyes, ears, touch. One lies, the other tells the truth. And sometimes they all lie, so you keep looking."

The remark had hardly left Nolan's mouth when the boat's world went white.

A crackle, a sharp cough like a small caliber shot, and a tongue of bright light leapt from the far end of the panel, so bright Mason flinched with his whole body. The smell hit a second later: burning insulation, a sweetness gone rancid. The light snapped off, leaving a scar on his vision.

"Kill power! Kill power to five!" the lead electrician snapped, calm but hard. His striker moved before the words finished, hand on the knife switch. The diving officer's head was already up. "What've you got?"

"Short on the five-bus feeder," the electrician said. "No fire visible."

His hands moved without looking: feel the panel front — hot. Not *burning* hot. He nodded once.

"Clear the deck around the panel. Nolan!"

"I'm here," Nolan said — he had already moved.

"Get me a CO_2 and stand by, but keep that bottle capped unless I say otherwise."

He turned to Mason.

The electrician's eyes cut to him, and for the first time since boarding the boat Mason felt a man measuring him and finding him either a help or a hazard.

"You. Runner, good. Tell engine room: hold load steady on motors — we've dropped five. Tell the mess: stay off the hotplate. Tell forward: battery ventilation to low; we may have a whiff of smoke and I don't want it chasing where I can't see it. Repeat it back."

Mason repeated it, breathless, and the man shook his head once. "Again, slower."

Mason slowed. He heard his own voice shape around the words and lodge them in his head. "Engine room hold load steady on motors, five is down. Mess stays off the hotplate. Forward sets battery ventilation to low."

"And tell control I'm isolating the section and will advise."

Mason ran.

Engine room first. The heat hit him like a wall, but the motors were only a background whine now; no diesels thundering meant he could be heard. He relayed the message. The engine room chief gave him the same two-finger heard you, then held up a palm steady and a thumb okay. No words, because none were needed when every man was fluent.

Mess next. "Mac! Stay off the hotplate, five is down."

Mac blinked, offended. "I'm not a fool, boy, I saw the flash from here." He clicked off two toggles with a practiced flick. "Get."

Forward. He banged a knee on the corner at the battery hatch, snarled under his breath, and kept moving. "Battery ventilation to low," he told a startled seaman, who relayed it down a ladder to a petty officer whose only response was to spin a wheel and kiss his teeth, as if he didn't like the taste of the air already.

Back to control. Nolan stood with the CO_2 already in his hands, cap still on, face blank. The electrician had the panel open fully now, and the light inside it was the light of a mouth, wires like teeth, a bite taken out of insulation black as a bruise.

"Section isolated," the electrician said, not looking up. "Short was here." He tapped a charred spot with a screwdriver. "We'll need a new run before we're happy. For now, I'll keep five dark and borrow from six to feed the essential."

"Do it," the diving officer said, and then raised his voice. "All stations: maintain reduced electrical load. We're proceeding on motors. That was not a drill. Good reactions. Keep them good."

A low murmur ran the length of the control room and out into the boat, acknowledgments, sighs, a curse from somewhere that sounded more awed than angry. Mason realized he had been breathing in short, shallow bursts and forced himself to pull one long draft of hot air.

Nolan leaned the CO_2 bottle back into its rack. "You see it?" he asked Mason, soft enough that only he could hear.

"I... saw the flash." Mason's mouth felt dry, his heart still up in his throat. He swallowed. "Smelled it too."

"What did it smell like?"

Mason blinked at him. "Burning insulation."

"What kind?"

He almost laughed. Then he saw Nolan wasn't smiling. He was serious with a fine seriousness that told Mason the answer mattered.

"Sweet," Mason said slowly. "Not like wood. Not like oil. Sweeter."

Nolan nodded. "Bakelite and rubber. You'll know it anywhere now. That smell means power eating itself somewhere you can't see yet. Chase it fast or the boat will fill with ghosts."

Mason looked down at his hands, which had trembled without his noticing. He clenched them once and let them go. "I was scared," he said. It felt like a confession.

"Good," Nolan said, and Mason jerked his head up at the word. "Fear makes you quick. Panic makes you stupid. You weren't stupid. You repeated the words right and brought back answers. That keeps men from dying."

Mason didn't know what to say to that, so he said nothing.

They ran without five for an hour while the electricians trimmed and replaced. The diving officer kept the drills off, as if to let the boat uncoil. Men returned to their stations. The motion of *Pike* settled into a tired sway, like a boxer between rounds.

When power was restored to the bus and the lead electrician said, "All right, bring her back up, gently," a small cheer went around the compartments. It wasn't loud. Submariners didn't cheer loud at anything that had teeth. But men breathed easier. The sweet stink in the air thinned.

"Back to work," the COB said in a voice that cut the cheer out of the air without cruelty. "Next drill in twenty."

Groans, real this time.

"Chief," the diving officer said to Nolan, "put your runner where he'll see the most and break the least."

"That's everywhere and nowhere," Nolan said, but there was humor under it. He jerked his chin at Mason. "You heard the man. You're mine until I'm sick of you."

They ran a fire drill in the after-torpedo room, rags in a bucket lit and smothered while men shouted the steps and timed how fast they could get a hose uncoiled and a nozzle seated. Mason carried words and wrenches, the world narrowing to tasks small and precise. They ran another flooding drill, this time in the engine room, where water spray on hot metal filled the air with a smell like pennies and steam. A planes jam drill followed, planesmen locking their wheels and shouting "Jammed!"

while the diving officer snapped commands and men spun handwheels on the standby rig until the bubble on the inclinometer stilled at zero.

Between each, Nolan quizzed him without warning: "Show me the forward battery air exhaust." "Trace that saltwater line with your finger without touching it." "If I told you to dog shut the number three watertight, where would your hands go first?"

The first time, Mason fumbled and pointed two frames off. Nolan grunted and tapped the right dogs with a knuckle. The next time, Mason slapped the correct dog without thinking and felt something shift inside him: not pride, not exactly, but the sense of a door unlocked in a corridor he hadn't known existed.

By late afternoon Mason's legs ached and his throat was raw from shouting messages over machinery. Sweat had drawn lines through the grime on his face. The swell had flattened a hair, or maybe he'd learned the roll. He realized, with a little shock, that he hadn't thought about puking in hours.

"Outboard horizon," the OOD called from the conning tower platform. "Destroyer two points off the bow, range twelve thousand and closing. We'll give him a peek-a-boo."

"Periscope drill," the diving officer said, almost cheerful. "Stand by."

They cycled through the dance: "Rig for depth." Lights down, voices down. "Take her down." The hiss of flooding, the hum of motors digging them under. The periscope rose like a metal flower through the tight throat of the well. The OOD's hands settled on the grips with a kind of tenderness.

"Down bubble two," the diving officer murmured. "Planes answer."

"Answering."

"Level her at sixty."

"Sixty feet, aye."

The OOD's shoulders turned slowly, his boots set wide, the scope cutting a slow circle that made Mason dizzy just to watch. "Scope up... down." Up and down, a stitch in a seam. The destroyer was out there somewhere, a gray knife that would swat them aside if they were clumsy. Mason's mouth dried again, but this time not from fear; from focus. It felt like eavesdropping on a conversation between predators.

"Good," the OOD said at last, voice neutral. "He never saw us. Secure from drill."

Lights back up a hair. Men returned to breathing. Somewhere aft Mac banged a lid and swore at beans.

Nolan looked at Mason. "You just watched the boat breathe."

Mason nodded, not trusting himself to say something that wouldn't sound foolish.

"You keep watching, you'll learn the rhythm. Then, when the rhythm's wrong, you'll feel it in your bones before the needles tell you. That's when you start being useful."

"I want to be useful," Mason said, the words out before he could stop them.

Nolan's face softened by a fraction. "You will be. The boat has a way of making use of men. Or she spits them back to the pier. Your choice which one you let her do."

They surfaced at dusk to charge batteries. The diesels roared back to life with an eager bellow that shook crockery and rattled teeth. Mason climbed to the bridge on Nolan's nod and watched the sea go from steel to ink to star-pocked glass. Far on the horizon a destroyer's running lights stitched a neat line. The air was cold and clean, and he drank it like water after a march.

"Better than the mess deck, eh?" Nolan murmured behind him.

Mason smiled, surprised to find there was energy left for the muscles of his face. "Yes, Chief."

"You didn't puke tonight," Nolan observed.

"No, Chief."

"You didn't die."

"No, Chief."

"And when the bus flashed you didn't run the wrong way."

"No... Chief."

"Then you're learning." Nolan's tone made the word carry the weight of a coin pressed into a palm. "Don't let it go to your head. Tomorrow we'll find a new way to scare you."

Mason looked out over the dark. "Chief?"

"Mm?"

"When the short hit... I smelled it. Before my eyes caught up. Sweet, like you said. Is that what you meant about the boat talking?"

Nolan's silence was a kind of approval. "That's part of it. She talks in smells and shivers, in little noises that don't belong. Most men never learn to listen. The ones who do last longer."

They stood without speaking for a long moment while the wind skinned their faces and the diesel exhaust blew aft in warm, oily sheets. The tender's distant lights were a memory; the shoreline a smear. The only solid, sure thing in a hundred miles of water was the little space of steel under their boots and the men inside it.

Mason thought of Groton, of the escape tank and the cold river and the instructors saying things that sounded like superstition. He had not believed any of it then. He wasn't sure he believed it now. But as *Pike* shouldered the swell and the diesels beat a steady heart, he felt something like trust take root. Not in miracles. In practice. In repetition. In hands on wheels and eyes on needles and noses smelling trouble before it bloomed.

He was exhausted enough to sleep on a line, but when he dropped into his rack that night, the boat's sounds weren't frightening. They were familiar. The faint chuff of a blower. The creak where the forward frames always complained when she took a sea on the port bow. The tick of a cooling pipe that reminded him, absurdly, of grasshoppers at dusk in Illinois.

He closed his eyes and saw the flash again, the white arc, the electrician's hands, Nolan's CO_2 steady and capped. His stomach flinched, but less than before. He let the picture run to the end, where it always had not just an ending but a lesson: smell, see, move, report, breathe.

Pike hummed around him.

Tomorrow there would be more drills. There would be new humiliations, new bruises, new words to get wrong. There might be another flash, or a spray, or a tilt that felt like falling off the world. But for the first time since stepping aboard he believed, quietly and without ceremony, that when the boat demanded more of him, he could answer with something other than fear.

He rolled on his side and tugged the curtain. The mess deck's lamp glowed dim beyond, a little amber star. A voice, someone's, drifted soft as a lullaby: "Reveille's at five, boys. Sleep while you can."

Mason smiled into the dark where no one could see it.

"Aye," he whispered to no one and to the boat. "Aye."

Pike returned to San Diego with her tanks low and her crew tired. The drills had wrung sweat from every man aboard, but there was a quiet satisfaction in it too. When the last line was made fast to *Holland*'s cleats, Mason felt his legs wobble, not from the swell this time, but from relief.

He'd survived.

While the others joked and hurried ashore, Mason lingered on the deck, one hand brushing the coaming of the hatch. Now that he'd been to sea, he wanted to understand this strange, unforgiving machine that carried them.

Pike was no battleship or cruiser. She was one of the Navy's new fleet submarines, Porpoise-class, built in the lean years of the mid-1930s when money was scarce and treaties tight. She displaced just over 1,300 tons on the surface, 2,000 submerged. At a glance, she was ungainly: high conning tower, stubby deck gun, a hull not quite sleek enough to call graceful.

But she was a step forward. Unlike the old S-boats, *Pike* had real endurance. She could stretch 8,000 miles at cruising speed without fueling, a reach that mattered in a Pacific Ocean wide enough to swallow continents. Her diesels weren't elegant, but they were tough. Her electric motors whispered quieter than the older boats. She carried four tubes forward, two aft, and a dozen torpedoes to feed them.

The crew, fewer than sixty men, lived crammed into a steel cylinder only 300 feet long. Everything doubled as something else: mess tables as bunks, passageways as storage, torpedoes as bedfellows. Privacy didn't exist. A man was lucky if he had a locker big enough for his shaving kit.

Mason thought of the mess deck where he'd nearly drowned in spilled coffee, the control room where a single short could blind them, the torpedo room where spray had soaked the deck. Every inch of it mattered. Every inch was alive with danger and discipline.

The instructors back in Groton had spoken of the submarine service like a priesthood, reserved for men with strong backs and stronger nerves. Now Mason understood. *Pike* was no lifeless machine. She was a world entire, steel and rivets wrapped around the fragile lives inside her.

He ran a hand over the paint, chipped and scarred. Beneath his palm, he swore he could feel her hum even as her diesels wound down.

"You'll learn her ways," Nolan said, coming up behind him. "She's a Porpoise. First of her kind. Not as pretty as the new ones they're building, but she'll keep you alive if you respect her."

Mason nodded, not trusting words.

San Diego's hills gleamed golden in the sunset. Liberty lay ahead for the crew, a few days to stretch legs ashore, to drink, to forget the smell of oil and sweat. Mason would go too, but part of him already knew the truth: he belonged more to *Pike* now than he did to the land waiting beyond the pier.

Chapter 5
Securing Alongside

They came in at first light, *Pike* nosing back through a waking harbor that smelled of tar, tide, and yesterday's coal smoke drifting off the piers. The hills behind San Diego wore a soft gray, and the bay lay in long, easy folds. After two days of drills and sudden alarms, it felt like walking into a church before the service: quiet, expectant, half-lit.

"Stand by to surface and make the fo'c'sle ready," the OOD called, voice even as ever.

"Stand by," echoed through the control room, and a moment later the clean slap of air over steel told Mason they were up and riding light. Diesels coughed, caught, and then roared into that steady bass that rattled crockery and teeth and somehow made a man feel safe.

Mason braced at the ladder and looked up into weak dawn. Nolan jerked his chin. "Topside. We'll be coming alongside *Holland*. Mind your feet and your mouth."

"Aye, Chief."

They broke into the gray air. *Holland* floated in the bay like a block of city dragged out and set down on water, cranes idle in the dawn, hoses hanging like sleeping snakes. Her running lights winked lazily; a few early hands moved along her decks with the loose gait of men who knew there was all day yet to work.

"Lines ready!" came sharp from the bridge. The forward deck crew answered in a chorus that carried along the submarine's spine, voices clipped, confident. *Pike*'s bow edged toward the tender's flank, screws nibbling, rudder tick-ticking corrections. The harbor pilot aboard *Holland* stood with a mug and a wool cap, squinting down, uninterested as a cat.

"Fenders over!" the deck leader barked.

They went, rubber and canvas cylinders slapping the water before they rose against *Holland*'s steel. The gap narrowed to a breath. A boatswain's pipe trilled from the tender. Mason could feel the boat's tiny sidle as the helms answered small touches: a woman sliding into a narrow seat without jostling the next.

"Make fast spring line!"

The throw spun out perfect; line snaked, caught, bit. *Holland*'s men bent to the cleat, set, and the whole rhythm changed, movement turning into strain, strain into rest.

"Bow line!"

"Made!"

"Stern line!"

"Made!"

"Double up!"

Ropes creaked into their loads. Somewhere aft a fender chirped as it squashed. The diesels eased from chesty to idle to quiet, like a big dog going from growl to breath. Mason let out an exhale he hadn't known he was holding. The deck under his boots stopped being a suggestion and became a fact.

"Secure the bridge," the OOD said simply, and the spell broke with a hundred small noises.

Securing a boat, Mason learned, was the opposite of getting underway, but it was no less a choreography. Nolan didn't have to shout; he just started moving, and Mason kept a half-step off his shoulder.

"Shut and tag all the nonessentials," Nolan told him, already pulling a small roll of stiff tags from a pocket. "If it doesn't need juice while we're tied, it doesn't get it. We don't cook the boat while the men cook their brains ashore."

"Yes, Chief."

"Battery charge cycle goes to the tender schedule; you'll see the board. No heroics. We're guests on *Holland*'s power. You touch her switchboard, you die on principle." The faintest smile. "Or at least you wish you had."

They dropped below. The air had already changed, cooler, less alive. The boat, so noisy and sure last night, lay caught between beats now. Voices carried differently. Steel clicked as it lost heat.

"Control first," Nolan said. "Then forward. Then you make a mess that would shame a church lady, clean, not dirty."

They moved station to station, tagging switches, spinning dust caps onto the mouths of valves, noting readings with a stub pencil and Nolan's compact, illegible scrawl. At each panel, Nolan pointed with two fingers, and Mason echoed back.

"Gyro to standby, tagged."

"Sonar amp off, tagged."

"Motor controller number two, leave it where it is." Nolan's finger hovered a hair above the toggle. "Tender's going to want a diagnostic later. If you tag it wrong, you'll have three men screaming at you in three different dialects of angry."

"Yes, Chief."

Forward, the torpedo room breathed oil and cold iron. Men in rolled sleeves were already moving like ants over a carcass, covers off, wrenches out, casualty cards clamped to clipboards. A petty officer torpedoman with a pencil behind one ear glanced up and flicked two fingers in greeting. "Morning, Chief. We'll want *Holland* to run a bore scope on number two's shutter. She dragged."

"I heard her," Nolan said. "Put it on the list."

"On the list," the torpedoman said, which sounded like a prayer in a church Mason had not yet learned. He slid past Mason without touching him, somehow fitting through a space that had not looked big enough.

The mess already smelled like soap and burned bacon. Mac wore a clean apron that would be dirty by noon, scowling at a pan like it had insulted his mother. "If you don't scrub every pot in this galley until I can see my face," he announced without looking up, "I will inform the Almighty you are unfit for His heaven."

"Yes, Mac," Mason said automatically, and grabbed the stack nearest his hands.

Nolan's knuckles rapped lightly against Mason's shoulder. "Not yet. Walk the carpenter's shop with me. You'll learn how we don't lose fingers when we're tied up."

They squeezed into a space the size of a closet where a bench vise and a saw tried to occupy the same inch of air. Nolan ran his palm over the vise jaw, checking for burrs, stepped on a pedal to confirm the saw was locked and tagged. "Men get cocky in port," he said. "Boat makes them feel safe till she reminds them she has no sense of humor. We treat her like she's running even when she sleeps."

"Chief?" Mason said as Nolan scribbled another tag. "How long do we... secure? I mean, when do we go again?"

"When *Holland*'s finished poking her and the skipper's finished buying us trouble," Nolan said. "A few days, if we're blessed. Long enough for you to remember what the sun looks like and for the gang to get stupid and poor. Why?"

"I... don't know." Mason shifted his weight. "It's just, feels strange. Stopping."

"You won't say that once Mac turns you into his scullery slave. Now move."

If getting underway had made Mason feel like a tourist on his own boat, securing alongside made him a janitor. It wasn't glamorous, but it was everywhere. The mess deck turned into a parade ground for brooms and swabs. He hauled sack after sack of trash up the forward hatch, face full of the sweet-sour stink of food gone to memory. He learned the tender's garbage routine the right way this time, through *Holland*'s detail, who relayed instructions with the bored authority of men who had said the same thing for ten years.

"No loose in the scow," one of them said, a big man with a belly like a buoy and hands like dock fenders. "Bag tight, knot tight, no glass where the rats can get at it." He glanced at Mason's collar. "*Pike*, eh? You boys always come back with twice as much garbage as you left with."

Mason managed a smile. "We make our own."

"Everyone does," the man said philosophically, and went back to smoking while he watched sailors do work.

Lines of men clomped past Mason carrying coils of hose, crates of spares from *Holland*'s stores, sealed tins heavy with the comfortingly anonymous promise of canned peaches. The tender smelled like a machine shop washed in coffee. The first time he crossed her quarterdeck that morning, the OOD gave him a flat look and Mason gave the ritual words back without tripping on them. The officer's mouth twitched a millimeter. Permission granted. He felt absurdly proud for stepping through a doorway correctly.

Back aboard, Nolan had him wipe down the control room panels with a rag barely damp, a fingertip's worth of oil to make the black paint glow.

"Don't flood it," Nolan said. "You're cleaning the skin of a cat. Stroke, don't soak."

Mason worked slow, savoring the tiny restoration, the way dust turned to sheen, the way his own face warped and slid across the curve of a gauge glass. He found his reflection in the depth gauge's lens and snorted under his breath at how young he looked with grime washed off.

"Pretty thing," the planesman said from the wheel, not looking up. "You gonna take that gauge dancing?"

Mason flushed. "Just making it... right."

"That's the word," the planesman said. "Make it right. Ten thousand wrongs every day; we make enough right to keep the boat alive."

He did the bulkheads in long strokes, the overhead with a rag tied around a stick so he wouldn't smear his hair with oil. Then the little stuff. Polished the periscope well with a rag until it felt warm under his palm. Wiped the brass plaque that named the builder and the year she'd gone down the ways. 1935. Not old, not new, middle-aged for a boat, he guessed; old enough to have opinions, young enough to surprise you.

"Mac wants you," someone grunted, and Mason obeyed.

For two hours he was a potato machine. Peel, dunk, peel, dunk, knuckles scoured white by soap and motion. Mac judged each spud like a gem cutter. "That one'll sprout in the pan, messman, do it again. That one's a poem. That one's a crime." His voice could flay and praise in the same breath.

When Mason hauled a pan to the sink and set it down a little too hard, the pot rang, and Mac's eyes flicked up. "Careful," he said quietly.

"Sorry," Mason muttered, muscles aching.

"You're not sorry yet. Care is how we live long enough to be sorry later. Lift with your legs."

Mason did.

Between trips he stole seconds to look down the length of the boat. With the engines quiet and the motors at rest, *Pike*'s noises were intimate: a tick from the forward frames as the sun warmed her skin on one side, a sigh from a valve packing that Nolan would probably hear and tighten with an eighth turn, a murmur of men telling the same shore stories a different way because they always ended in laughter.

He wasn't sure when it happened, but he realized the sting of being "fresh fish" had faded to an itch. Men still called him messman, but some of them said it without teeth. The planesman had called his wiping "right." Mac had called one of his potatoes a poem, even if he'd flayed the next three. Nolan, well, Nolan never praised out loud, but he hadn't stopped him every minute, and sometimes that was praise.

They checked the watch bill tacked on a clipboard near the control room hatch. Liberty details were penciled in blocks. Shore patrol would sweep the streets tonight, tomorrow, and the day after in regular tides. The names next to "liberty" tickled the inside of Mason's ribs with a nervous itch. His was there, in the second wave. He traced it with a clean finger, more to feel the letters than to read them.

"Don't spend it all at the first bar," Nolan said over his shoulder, as if he'd been reading Mason's mind as easily as the paper.

"How many bars does it take?" Mason asked, surprising himself by joking.

"All of them," Nolan said, deadpan. Then, after a beat: "And it still won't be enough to make you smarter. So stop after two."

"Two what?"

"Good decisions," Nolan said. "The drinks will take care of themselves."

By midafternoon, *Pike* was as squared away as she ever got in port. *Holland*'s gang clanged a portable brow down, and a stream of tradesmen in clean dungarees came aboard with kits like doctors' bags. An electrician from the tender, older, with eyes that missed nothing, stood shoulder-to-shoulder with *Pike*'s own lead and looked into the panel that had coughed light the day before.

"There," the tender man said, tapping the char with a screwdriver the way the *Pike* electrician had. "Chafed under a clamp. She was going to bite you sooner or later."

"Sooner," *Pike*'s man said. "She chose sooner."

"A favor," the *Holland* man said. "You smelled her, didn't you?"

"Everyone did," *Pike*'s man said, and his eyes cut sideways just enough to brush Mason. It wasn't praise exactly, but it was acknowledgment, and Mason tucked it away like a confiscated coin.

In the forward room, a tender machinist with the patience of a saint ran a borescope into the shutter track of number two tube while two torpedomen watched like students. The screen showed a thin, bright tunnel, the world reduced to circles and scratches.

"There," the machinist murmured. "A burr. She dragged. You try to slam that shut in a hurry and it'll stick just when you need it not to. You dress it with love, not a hammer."

"I like hammers," one torpedoman confessed.

"I can tell, by your face," the machinist said without malice, and Mason swallowed a laugh.

In the mess, Mac fed the tender's fitters coffee as if it were communion. *Holland*'s men drank without comment, which was a kind of compliment. Mac's eyes slid to Mason for a half second, see?, and then away, as if lessons were always happening whether or not anyone named them.

When Nolan finally let Mason sit, it was on a coil of line under the open hatch where the warm, thin sunlight came down like a visit from another planet. Mason pressed his back to the bulkhead and shut his eyes for a count of ten, and that was enough to make him feel the boat under him again: not swaying now, just breathing.

"Don't fall asleep there," Nolan said. "COB will step on you."

"I'm awake," Mason said, though the gravity that pulled at him felt like a hand behind his neck.

"You're learning," Nolan said, as if continuing a conversation they'd been having since Mason stepped aboard. "And the boat noticed."

Mason opened one eye. "How do you know?"

"She didn't kill you," Nolan said simply. "That's usually her first hello."

Mason snorted. "That what you tell all the new men?"

"That's what I tell the ones who look like they're listening." Nolan nudged the coil with his toe. "Up. Go steal ten minutes on *Holland*'s weather deck. Breathe some air that doesn't taste like coffee and old socks.

Then come back and make Mac proud before he makes you cry."

Mason got to his feet. "Aye, Chief."

Holland felt like shore planted on water. Her deck was wide as a county road. Hawsers bigger around than Mason's thigh lay coiled like sleeping pythons. Somewhere amidships a whistle blew and a petty officer's voice rattled through a speaking tube, orders flying to some unseen party. Men in clean blue worked with the economy of habit, painting, splicing, checking, signing.

Mason drifted to the rail and looked down. *Pike* lay pressed to *Holland*'s side like a child asleep with a hand on its mother's shirt. From this angle, she looked impossibly small. He could see the curve of her back, the line where light made a narrow gleam along the top of her hull. Scars in the paint showed where a thousand feet had passed. The after flag hung limp in the noon lull.

The big bay looked gentle, but a tug trundled past with a barge on a hawser and the wake slapped at *Pike*'s side with a flat hand. Fenders squeaked. The submarine rolled a fraction, enough to make the flag give a single lazy lift.

"Pretty, ain't she?" said a voice at his elbow. It was the tender deckhand with dock-fender hands who'd ridden the garbage detail earlier. He held his cigarette like a man who had been told to quit and compromised by smoking only half.

"Pretty," Mason agreed.

"You're on her, they said," the man went on. "Fresh. You'll either love it or curse it. Sometimes both same minute."

"Which did you do?" Mason asked.

"Loved it," the man said, surprising him. "Then I got tired of not seeing sky and moved over here. But some mornings..." He exhaled smoke. "Some mornings I miss that feeling when she settles under and the noise changes. Like shutting a door on the world."

Mason didn't realize he'd been smiling until the man grinned back. "You know it already."

"I think I do."

"Keep your head. Don't make your mama cry. And when you go ashore, keep your shoes tied."

"My shoes?"

"Bar fights," the man said blandly. "Things get sticky on the floor, laces catch, and then you're dancing without meaning to. Saves lives, tied shoes."

"I'll remember," Mason said, serious as church, and the man laughed softly and clapped his shoulder.

"Good kid."

Back aboard *Pike*, the afternoon tilted toward evening. The watch bill went up for real this time, not in pencil. The OOD read it once out loud in the control room, and men listened even if they pretended not to, because a list was a promise and a warning. Mason's name sat beside a time that meant he had a few more hours of work and then, freedom. The word felt both enormous and thin.

"Nolan," the COB said from the hatch with a voice that carried authority without volume, "make sure your pup knows how to sign out and back in. Don't have *Holland* send me a telegram asking if we've lost any of our children."

"I'll walk him, COB," Nolan said.

"And don't let Mac feed the tender's whole repair party out of our larder," the COB added to the air, and from the galley Mac's voice sailed back, wounded and righteous: "As if I would ever!"

Men chuckled. The COB's mouth might have moved half a millimeter. It was, Mason was beginning to understand, the submarine version of a broad smile.

They finished the last of the tags, chalked a neat column of "SECURED" beside a list of systems that earlier in the day had been hungry and loud, and Nolan stepped back to admire the tidy murder of work.

"Looks like a boat," he said. "Let's keep her that way."

He flicked his eyes at Mason. "Uniform checks. Shore patrol likes to make examples of fresh faces."

Mason smoothed his jumper, checked buttons, made sure his hat sat square and low. Nolan tugged at a collar point with the casual intimacy of a man setting a rifle sight.

"Good enough," he pronounced. "You'll still look like a

baby to the girls and a payday to the barkeeps. Try not to break. Try not to make promises you can't keep."

"Two good decisions," Mason said, remembering.

"Now you're getting it."

Nolan's gaze slid once along the boards, the valves, the quiet instruments. He touched the periscope well with a knuckle the way some men touch a doorway on their way out, habit, superstition, respect.

"Permission to go ashore will be granted from the quarterdeck at the tender," he recited for Mason's benefit. "You'll ask. You'll be granted. You'll walk down that gangway like a man who remembers where his other home is."

"I will," Mason said.

"And when you come back," Nolan added, voice a shade softer, "you'll ask again. Because the words matter. Because the boat hears them even when she pretends not to."

Mason nodded. "Aye, Chief."

"Go peel two more pans for Mac," Nolan said briskly, as if slicing sentiment out of the air. "Then you can think about what foolishness to commit on my time."

Mason grinned and headed for the galley, light on his feet in a way he would not have thought possible a week ago. He passed the depth gauge and could not help himself, he touched the rim of the glass with the pad of his finger, a quick, private salute. The boat was quiet and busy, like a woman cleaning her hair after a long day. Men moved inside her with purpose and affection. Outside, the harbor burned brighter, the sky turning the color of peaches in syrup.

It would all come undone in a few hours, liberty bells, laughter, bar lights, music, trouble. Chapter four's second part was already spilling toward them like tide.

But for this hour, *Pike* was squared away, tied to her mother ship, alive and resting. Mason's name was on the bill. His shoes were tied. The seabag he hadn't touched since parting with it at the hatch sat under his rack like a reminder and a promise.

He picked up Mac's pan and scrubbed, and the rhythm of it, the circle, the rinse, the circle, felt, unexpectedly, like belonging.

The first liberty bell was struck in the late afternoon, and *Pike*'s crew flowed toward *Holland*'s quarterdeck like water seeking a gap. Mason went with them, jumper scrubbed, shoes shined, hat square. He had rehearsed the words Nolan drilled into him: Request permission to go ashore, sir. Simple enough, but with the tender's topside men glaring down their noses, it felt like a final exam.

The *Holland*'s quarterdeck watch scanned each liberty pass as though they were entry tickets to heaven. "Next. Pass." A surface sailor with a permanent sneer snapped Mason's chit, looked at his baby face, and drawled, "Submarines letting schoolboys aboard now?"

The men behind Mason chuckled, some not kindly, but Mason held his salute and repeated the words clear. He wasn't going to give the man the satisfaction.

The OOD flicked two fingers. "Permission granted."

Mason stepped smartly across and let his breath go only when his boots hit the brow.

Behind him someone muttered, "Better than I did my first time."

It was Jensen, a wiry signalman striker from *Pike* who had a permanent half-smile and a talent for poker Mason had already learned to avoid. Jensen slapped Mason's shoulder. "Don't worry about the tender swabs. They think they're Navy royalty 'cause they've got bunks bigger than coffins."

"Let 'em have their bunks," another voice put in, O'Hara, a torpedoman second class from New Jersey, broad and bluff. "They don't ride into the drink with a hundred feet of water over their heads. They can keep their clean uniforms and smug faces."

The three fell in together, cutting through *Holland*'s broad decks to the shore-side landing. The late sun shone off the water, where launches bobbed like impatient horses waiting for a whip.

The launch's coxswain counted heads and waved them down into benches that stank of bilge and salt. They shoved off with a groan of wood and splash of oars before the engine caught.

The ride was quick, but Mason noticed every detail: the harbor widening, the forest of masts and funnels, the tender growing huge and gray behind them. Other launches passed, loaded with sailors laughing and already shouting about bars and women. One of the boats nearly swamped itself when someone leaned too far trying to light a cigarette.

"Don't fall overboard, Mason," Jensen quipped. "You'll never live it down."

The launch nudged into the landing pier. A crowd of sailors in uniform already waited, men from cruisers, destroyers, a few from the carrier riding out deeper. The smell of the shore reached them: dust, gasoline, fried tortillas, perfume on the breeze.

Shore patrol moved among the sailors, white belts and pistols, keeping order. A petty officer barked at a pair of destroyer hands for open containers, cuffed one lightly on the head, and sent them marching on.

Mason straightened his jumper again. "They check liberty passes here too?"

"Sometimes," O'Hara said. "Mostly just looking for troublemakers and drunks. You'll know when they want you. Don't give 'em a reason."

"Best advice you'll get all night," Jensen added. "Now let's find a bus to Tijuana before every other fool in San Diego beats us there."

The bus rattled south along the dusty highway, springs squealing with every bump. The windows were open, the air a hot slap of dust and gasoline, and the bench seat Mason shared with O'Hara and Jensen vibrated like a loose deck plate. The bus smelled of cigarettes and wool uniforms that had already soaked up a day's worth of sweat.

"This your first liberty, Mason?" Jensen asked, tipping his cap back just enough to reveal his permanent smirk.

Mason nodded. "First since Groton. Just a couple nights in New London before we shipped west."

"New London," O'Hara chuckled. "That ain't liberty, that's charity. You can't call it liberty until you've woken up in Tijuana with a wallet light, a head heavy, and a shore patrolman telling you to move along."

Mason gave a thin smile. "Guess I'll try not to make it that far."

"Oh, you will," Jensen said. "Everybody does, once. Question is whether you learn something after."

The bus jolted into a rut, and O'Hara planted a big hand against the seatback to steady himself. "What's your story, Mason? Don't tell me you came straight outta some naval academy. You don't look the type."

"Farm," Mason said simply. "Illinois. Corn, pigs, a couple milk cows. I worked it with my father and brothers 'til I enlisted."

Jensen arched an eyebrow. "A farm boy? No wonder you look surprised every time a valve hisses. You still expecting cows to wander out of the torpedo room?"

The men around them laughed. Mason flushed but kept his voice even. "Cows don't try to kill you when you forget to check a breaker. *Pike* does."

O'Hara grinned. "He's not wrong."

They bumped along in companionable noise, trading smokes, while the rest of the bus sang off-key Navy songs that bled into each other.

The Blue Whale was already overflowing by the time they pushed through its door. The bar reeked of beer and cigar smoke, the floor sticky under Mason's shoes. A brass band played with more volume than skill in the corner, and sailors shouted orders over one another in English and mangled Spanish.

They crammed into a table at the back, the wood scarred with carvings of initials and dates. A girl with dark hair and quick hands slid four bottles onto the table without asking.

"To *Pike*," O'Hara said, raising his.

"To *Pike*," they echoed.

Mason's first swallow was bitter and icy, hitting his stomach like cold iron. He coughed, choking, and Jensen thumped his back hard enough to rattle his teeth.

"Farm boy doesn't know beer," Jensen teased.

"I know beer," Mason said when he could breathe again. "Just not this kind."

"Out there you probably drank corn liquor from a mason jar," O'Hara said.

Mason hesitated. "Sometimes."

That sent them roaring again. Mason laughed along, feeling the knot in his stomach ease.

Later, with the first bar behind them and a little warmth from the drink in his veins, Mason found himself listening more than speaking as his shipmates traded stories.

Jensen leaned close, his voice pitched over the noise of the street. "Me, I'm Brooklyn born. Old man worked the docks 'til he broke his back. I wasn't gonna haul crates for nickels, so I signed the papers. Better to swab decks in blues than rot in grease at home."

O'Hara snorted. "At least you had a choice. Jersey wasn't any better. My old man drank himself to the grave when I was fifteen, and Ma told me there was no food for a grown boy with a mouth like mine. Navy took me in before the cops did." He said it with a kind of grin, but Mason heard the truth under it.

They looked at Mason. "So? What made you leave the farm?"

Mason stared at the street ahead, lamps buzzing, the press of uniforms all around. "I didn't want to spend the rest of my life behind the same plow. My brothers will run the farm fine without me. I wanted to see the ocean. To do something that mattered." He paused, embarrassed by his own honesty. "Guess I found more ocean than I expected."

There was a beat of silence, then O'Hara grinned and clapped him on the shoulder. "That's as good a reason as any, farm boy. You'll fit in fine."

Jensen nodded, his smirk softer this time. "A man who listens more than he talks lasts longer under the sea."

The Foreign Club was bigger, brighter, and twice as noisy. Neon beer signs glowed over polished bars. Mexican and American flags hung side by side. The band here was better, brass horns cutting through the roar of sailors packed shoulder-to-shoulder.

Mason watched as his shipmates scattered: Jensen to a poker table, O'Hara to the dance floor. Mason nursed his beer, trying not to look as young as he felt.

A destroyer sailor leaned over, eyeing his dolphin-less chest. "Submarine man, huh? Thought you boys were all ghosts. What's it like, stuffed in a tube?"

"Hot," Mason said honestly. "Loud. Smells like oil."

The man chuckled. "Smells like home, then. Cheers, fish."

Mason drank, realizing with a small surprise that the insult rolled off easier than it had aboard. Out here, on liberty, they were all just sailors burning pay.

At their third bar, trouble almost bloomed. A spilled drink between O'Hara and a destroyer sailor stiffened into a square-shouldered standoff. Mason's heart thudded, he imagined shore patrol's pistols, the brig, the COB's wrath.

Then Nolan was suddenly there, as if conjured from smoke. "Knock it off," he said flatly. No raised voice, no threat, but both men stepped back like boys caught fighting in church.

Nolan's eyes cut to Mason. "You keeping your head down?"

"Yes, Chief."

"Good. Keep it there."

By midnight, the streets thinned, sailors staggering toward the border. The last bus north had gone, and Mason found himself with Jensen, O'Hara, and Nolan trudging along the dusty road under flickering lamps.

They passed a group of Marines singing off-key, shore patrol hovering like sheepdogs. Mason's feet ached in his shoes, but he remembered Nolan's warning and kept his laces tight.

At the border, they handed over their liberty passes again, the guards barely glancing before waving them through. On the U.S. side, sailors sprawled on benches, some already asleep, some smoking the last of their pay away. A shore patrol officer muttered darkly about the first launches back to *Holland*, leaving at dawn.

"They don't run the launches all night?" Mason asked.

"Nope," O'Hara said, dropping onto a piling like a sack. "First boat at dawn. Get used to it, farm boy."

Officers passed now and then, noses wrinkled, muttering about "goddamned liberty men," but none stopped them.

"They hate seeing us here," Jensen added, stretching. "Say it looks undisciplined. But hell, better here than cooling your heels in Tijuana jail."

Mason leaned against the wood, exhausted. Across the bay, the tender's lights gleamed faintly. *Pike* was tied alongside, waiting. Despite the beer, the smoke, the dust, Mason felt something like warmth in his chest.

For the first time, he wasn't just a mess cook fumbling in the dark. He was part of a crew with names, stories, scars. He was beginning to belong.

The pier was quiet now, save for the occasional snore from the sailors sprawled across benches and bollards. The lamps buzzed faintly. Beyond the dark water, *Holland*'s bulk loomed, her deck lights haloed in mist. *Pike* was invisible from here, but Mason knew exactly where she lay tied, pressed against her tender's side like a child against its mother.

Mason sat with his back against a piling, cap tilted low, too tired to sleep. Beside him, Nolan smoked in silence, the glow of his cigarette a steady pulse against the dark.

"Chief?" Mason said after a long while.

"Mm."

"What's *Pike* really for? I mean... we do drills, we train, but what's the point? She doesn't feel like the big ships."

Nolan exhaled smoke slowly, watching it curl. "You're not wrong. She's no battleship. Navy brass still argue about what to do with us. Some think we're scouts. Some think we're commerce raiders. Some think we're toys to scare the Japanese with."

"The Japanese?" Mason asked.

"You heard the news same as me," Nolan said. "China's burning. Japan's taking bites out of it and won't stop until somebody slaps their hand. That somebody's likely us. Mark me, someday soon these fleet boats won't be just drilling off San Diego. They'll be over there, in the Philippines and further west, keeping an eye on the Rising Sun."

Mason swallowed. "You really think so?"

Nolan ground out the cigarette. "I know so. The admirals might pretend otherwise, but I've been around long enough to smell where the wind's blowing." He looked at Mason. "That's why you learn every inch of that boat now. Because one day soon, it won't be practice anymore."

The words sat heavy between them. Mason tried to imagine *Pike* pushing west across the Pacific, into waters he couldn't even picture, hunting Japanese ships. He thought of the drills, the alarms, the way his heart had pounded when the short circuit flashed. He thought of whether he'd be ready.

"Were you always on subs?" he asked, if only to keep from dwelling on it.

Nolan's mouth tugged sideways. "No. Destroyers first. Ran out of Norfolk, chased smugglers in the Caribbean. Good duty for a young fool. But the sea pounds you raw on a tin can. Subs... well, they pound you too, but in different ways.

Quieter ways. I came to *Pike* when she was new. I've seen her through four skippers and God knows how many green messmen like you."

He gave Mason a look that was half stern, half fond. "Some washed out. Some made rate and stayed. A few never came back from dives. Boat doesn't care which. She just wants men who listen."

Mason nodded slowly. "And you stayed."

"I stayed," Nolan said simply. He looked out over the water again, voice softer. "Because down there, it's just us and the boat. No admirals, no brass bands, no one to save you but yourself and the men beside you. It's honest."

For a while, neither spoke. The first light of dawn began to gray the eastern sky. Gulls wheeled over the landing, calling sharp and hungry.

A launch engine coughed to life down the pier, and sailors stirred, groaning, stretching, rubbing eyes. Mason stood, feeling the stiffness in his legs, and looked at Nolan.

"Chief?"

"Mm."

"I don't want to be the one who screws it up out there."

Nolan snorted. "Then don't. Not complicated." He flicked his cigarette butt into the water.

The launch bumped against the landing. Men shuffled aboard, some still half asleep, some already cracking jokes. Mason followed Nolan down, boots on the wet planks.

As the boat puttered back across the harbor, Mason looked toward *Holland* and the shape he knew was *Pike*, waiting. For the first time, he didn't see just steel and rivets. He saw a future stretching further west than he had ever dreamed.

Chapter 6
Leaving the Comfort Zone

Orders came down just after dawn: *Pike* would join fleet problems up the coast, winter water, hard drills. The words ran through the compartments faster than a messenger, men repeated them the way farmers repeat weather, with fatalism and a little relish.

Mason felt the change before the lines were even in. The air had a bite that found his ears and stayed there, and the bay's lazy chop wore a darker shade. The tender's cranes stood like gray gallows against the pale sky. On *Pike*'s deck, oilskins appeared, collars rose, and jokes thinned to grunts.

"Cast off," the OOD called, voice carrying clean as a bell over the small deck.

Lines snapped free one after the other. Fenders squeaked, breath fogged, boots thudded. *Pike* edged from *Holland*'s side, nosed into the channel like a wary animal. Diesels came up with a cough and then a steady, chest-deep chant that set every plate in the mess a-quiver.

Mason stood topside long enough to taste the morning, tar, cold iron, the stale coffee breath of the harbor, before Nolan's chin flick sent him below.

"Enough sky. You'll get your fill of it soon."

"Feels colder already," Mason said, dropping through the hatch into air that smelled like warm machinery and wool.

Nolan's mouth crooked. "That's because it is."

The breakwater threw its last polite wave beneath *Pike*'s bow and then the Pacific took over. It came in long-shouldered swells that lifted the boat's nose and laid it down with an iron hand. On the surface, green water came flat and hard, over the deck, over the bridge, then ran away laughing. Submerged, the motion found the boat anyway, a slow, relentless heave that rattled cups and tested knees.

Mason carried coffee to the control room and learned afresh what "slosh" meant. Half a mug scalded his wrist, and he bit his jaw to keep from yelping. The diving officer took his cup with a nod that might have been thanks, and Nolan, braced in a corner like a tree with a low center of gravity, tilted his head.

"Knees," Nolan said. "Give them to the boat. Lock them and you'll go over like a fencepost."

Mason unlocked his knees and felt the truth of it immediately, his weight found a path through him into the deck, into the boat itself. The roll still came, but now it flowed around him like a river around a rock.

"Better," Nolan said, eyes already cataloging gauges.

Back in the mess, Jensen's grin hung upside down from the bunk above the table. "How's the farm, Mason? Crops look good?"

"Crops are underwater," Mason said, clutching the table's edge as the boat took a longer, meaner lurch.

"Sunshine Navy," O'Hara announced to no one, shouldering through with a pan like a shield. "That's what they call San Diego duty. This, " the hull groaned under a breaking sea ", is the Navy's winter teeth."

The galley became a theater of sliding pans and swearing. Mac had lashed his stove with ropes like taming a mule; the pot lids clattered a rhythm all their own. He cooked as if the sea were a personal insult.

"Eat," he commanded, slapping a plate in front of Mason without slowing. "You puke it up? Fine. But you put something in first."

Mason stared at beans shiny with grease and bread that looked like ballast. He made himself fork a bite and found, to his surprise, that hunger and nausea could coexist like enemies on a train, one scowling, the other doing business anyway. He kept it down. Barely.

"Attaboy," Jensen murmured.

The boat taught with bruises. Mason learned exactly how high to lift his foot to clear the coaming when the deck rolled the wrong way. He learned the sharp report of his hipbone against the mess seat when he misjudged timing by half a second. He learned the smell of his own sleeve burned by hot coffee, and how to carry the next tray with his hand under the lip, not out at the side like a flag.

He also learned that in heavy water, everything tried to escape its assigned place. He and a junior electrician spent an hour putting the world back where it belonged: lashing the bread locker, re-wedging the potato crate, pinning a toolbox that had ambitions of migration.

"Why's it even back here?" Mason asked, yanking a line tight.

The electrician, a slight man with careful hands, shrugged. "Because a man set it here when the sea was nice. The sea's not nice now. Remember that."

They did an after-lunch tour with Nolan, and now Mason's ears had work to do. The hull had a new voice in cold water, lower, with more complaint in the bones. Bolts pinged occasionally as the pressure loaded and unloaded them, and somewhere a stanchion creaked because it had a dry squeak that hadn't been there yesterday.

"What's that?" Nolan asked, not pointing, because Nolan never pointed at the answer.

Mason let the noise roll around in his head. "Not a pump. Not a man. High, no, not high. Sharp."

"Sharp's right," Nolan said. "Lose that squeak and you'll hunt for what changed. You're not hunting it now because

I told you it's fine. But the boat won't tell you next time. She'll just stop squeaking and start leaking."

They paused by the forward battery hatch. A line on a gauge jittered in the low end of acceptable. Nolan tapped the glass with a knuckle.

"What's that tell you?"

"Cold," Mason ventured. "She's colder."

"She's colder," Nolan agreed. "Cold's honest. Engines will lie to you before cold does. Write it down anyway."

Mason wrote it down. Writing it made it real, the way tying a knot made a rope belong to a cleat.

By night, *Pike* was a metal coffin rocking in the dark with a bad temper. Mason lay in his rack and let the boat's complaints become a map. The long groan when they took a wave on the port bow. The little rattle in the overhead that must be a light fixture whispering to itself. The deep hum that meant the motors were bearing them along submerged with patience.

He slept in slices: ten minutes with his mouth open, twenty with his jaw clenched, seven dreaming of wheat bending to wind that felt too wet. Waking came like standing up from a fall he hadn't realized he'd taken.

A hand shook his shoulder, Nolan's, because Nolan shook like a machine: twice, exact, firm. "Messenger," he said, and in that word was duty and mercy both. The mercy was that messenger duty meant moving, and moving was better than laying still pretending not to be tired.

In the control room, the air was warmer. The diving officer's pencil ticked like a metronome across a clipboard. The planesmen had their hands light on the wheels, their eyes on bubbles. The OOD's cap brim made a dark line over a face that seemed incapable of surprise.

"Engine room, hold steady at present load," the diving officer said, and Mason repeated it back to Nolan and then to the engine room chief, whose two fingers to the temple meant heard and acknowledged. The words passed through Mason and came back, and for once he didn't feel like a kink in the hose; he felt like part of the hose.

"Forward room, stand by to shift trim aft one percent." He ran the message, dodging one man, pivoting around another. His shoulder brushed the periscope well, warm where a dozen hands had rested earlier. The forward watch nodded sharp, spun a wheel with a sure hand, and Mason took that yes back along the artery to control.

"Messenger," Nolan said, the word a summons and a test. "Tell Mac to keep the hotplate cold till we bring the lights down. We'll need the amps."

"Mac, hotplate, lights down," Mason said, trotting to the mess. He got a pan lid thrown at his head for the trouble, but the lid missed and Mac's hand hit the switch anyway.

"Tell your boss I like him as much as I like the sea," Mac grumbled, and Mason carried the sentiment back with the message because every word mattered when spoken between tight spaces.

He learned the dive room's particular smell when bodies warmed it and pumps were working: wool, hot dust, a living animal smell that wasn't quite sweat. He learned the way men handed him space because he wore messenger on his face, and the way they didn't move if he wasn't clear, because movement got you killed if it wasn't right.

During a particularly savage roll, the clipboard tried to leave his hand. He caught it to his chest without losing the pencil. Nolan's eyes touched him once and moved on, but Mason felt the touch like a coin set on his palm.

They surfaced in sleet. The watch bill sent Mason topside to help lash a line that had chafed and gone slack. The ladder rung felt like a bayonet. He came out into air that carved his lungs from the inside, and the world became spray, gray sky, and the bow's pure white slash through dirty water.

"Clip in," the bridge watch snapped, and Mason fumbled his carabiner onto the safety line. Gloves turned him clumsy, but he got it, felt the solid bite of metal to metal, and edged down the side deck. The rail was slick with a skin of ice. He set both boots with thought, crouched when the next sea shouldered over, took it on his back, shook like a dog, moved again.

Beside him, O'Hara sang tunelessly just to have something in his mouth that wasn't cold air. "Ain't she a beauty?" he hollered.

Mason would later swear O'Hara grinned in sleet. "She's something," he yelled back, and meant it. The line's fibers were stiff as bone under his hands, the knot fat with ice. He worked his fingers numb and then found them warm again, a strange sensation of blood becoming belief. When the knot sat like it belonged there, he slapped it and nodded to the bridge. The acknowledgment came as a dipped hand. They scuttled back, crabwise, legs bent like sailors in a painting someone would never buy.

Below, the warmth felt indecent. His face stung as blood returned. Jensen reached up from his bunk with a towel and dropped it on Mason's head.

"Don't drip on my good shoes," Jensen said, which was a joke because Jensen's shoes were as bad as anyone's.

"You own shoes?" Mason asked through the towel.

"Borrowed 'em," Jensen said. "Same as everyone borrows everything on a boat."

"Give me that towel," O'Hara demanded, and then thwacked Mason's skull with the wet cloth because there wasn't a thing on earth O'Hara couldn't turn into a game for half a second.

"Grow up," Mac barked from the galley. "Or at least grow quiet."

Fatigue set in the way cold does: slowly, then all at once. Men's faces took on a smoky color, eyes bruised underneath. Voices shortened. Laughter came in bursts and snapped off like a valve shutting. A man slept on a coil of line because the distance to his rack felt like a foreign country. Someone wrote to a wife at the mess table, pencil making caves of words because the sea gave a slight chop even to handwriting.

Mason's fingers found their own little choreography: lay the cup here where it won't travel, put your hip there, slide the hatch one more inch so it won't bang when the roll catches it. He ducked without looking now. The pipe that had taught him its lesson three times got no more blood from him.

He watched Nolan watch the boat. The petty officer's eyes tracked things Mason could not see, engineer's numbers in his head, perhaps, or the shape of a noise. He had a way of putting his hand on the periscope well or the bulkhead without looking, a palm's worth of contact that said I know you. Once, in a quiet minute, Mason imitated it, splaying his hand on cool steel. The boat hummed under his palm, a purr low as an old cat's. He pulled his hand back quickly, embarrassed at the superstition of it, but less embarrassed than he would have been a month ago.

"What's that grin?" Jensen asked, flopping down beside him with a noise that would have toppled a less balanced man.

"Nothing," Mason said.

"Nothing," Jensen repeated in a falsetto. "That's the best part of boat life. A man starts smiling at bulkheads and nobody carts him away."

"You talk to your bunk," Mason said.

"My bunk and I have an understanding," Jensen replied. "It holds me up and I don't kick it."

"Messenger," Nolan said from the hatch, and the two men leapt because the word had a hook in it.

Late on the second night, the swell changed its mind. The boat's motion found a new angle; plates slid a new way; the ping in the overhead took a longer pause between notes. Mason felt it before anyone said it. He looked up from the mess table and saw O'Hara tilt his head like a dog. In control, the planesman's bubble took three beats to settle instead of two.

"Wind's veered," the OOD remarked to air that had ears.

Mason felt absurdly pleased with himself for noticing, and then felt childish for the pleasure. He pushed the feeling aside and got back to work.

When he finally crashed into his rack later that watch, he closed his eyes and saw not Illinois wheat or the blue ridge at the edge of his home fields, but the depth gauge's slow, stately needle, and the inclinometer bubble's intent wobble as hands built a level in a moving world. He dreamed of a pump's whisper, regular, honest, the sort of sound men live by.

He woke once to a bang that meant nothing, a dropped wrench amplified by steel, and once to a bang that meant something, forward, followed by a voice saying calmly, "Got it," which meant he could sleep again.

Morning coffee tasted like victory. It was burnt and strong and came in a mug with brown lines at the lip, but it warmed his hands and put shape in his head. Mac slid him a heel of bread with bacon stuck to it in a way that claimed accident and showed mercy.

"Eat that before I change my mind," Mac said. "You look like a ghost with a haircut."

"Thanks," Mason said, and the word had as much heft as anything else he'd carried.

"Don't thank me. Thank the pig," Mac said. "And my mother."

"Your mother?"

"For teaching me not to poison sailors," Mac said, deadpan, and slapped another pan onto a burner.

Nolan appeared with a clipboard and a pencil like he had been created with them. "Messenger."

Mason wiped his hands and stood.

"Remember what you learned yesterday," Nolan said, eyes steady. "Not the words. The listening. The boat changes up here, " he tapped Mason's temple ", before she changes down there." He jerked his chin at the deck.

Mason didn't have a clever answer. "Aye, Chief," he said simply.

He followed Nolan into control, set his boots where they belonged, unlocked his knees, and breathed with the boat. Outside, the ocean wore its winter face. Inside, *Pike* prepared to meet it without apology.

The swagger wasn't in Mason yet. But when the boat rolled, his body answered instead of complaining, and when a pan clanged or a gauge twitched, his head sorted noise from warning with less guesswork than before. He had bruises on bruises and a tiredness that made eyelids heavy even when he laughed, but a corner of him was waking to the rhythm Nolan had promised.

The fleet waited ahead, destroyers and guns and drills named like games. For now, Part I ended in motion, north, into rougher water, Mason steadying to a new beat, learning the first steps of the dance he'd have to know by heart.

Morning came gray and low, the sky a lid pressed over the Pacific. *Pike* rode the swell like a tired boxer, taking each punch with a grunt. Inside, the crew was restless. Even the jokes had worn thin.

"Fleet Problems," O'Hara muttered as he laced his boots on the mess bench. "Whoever named 'em never spent a night in this coffin rolling end to end."

"They don't name them for us," Jensen replied from his bunk, flipping a deck of cards idly. "They name them for the brass. Admirals get reports. We get bruises."

Mason sat on the edge of his rack, buttoning his jumper with stiff fingers. He had slept little, rocked awake by every pitch of the boat. His stomach had settled some since San Diego, but now his nerves replaced the seasickness. Drills meant movement, noise, the chance to stumble or freeze where everyone could see.

Nolan passed through, clipboard tucked under one arm, eyes scanning without pause. "On your feet, Mason. Fleet's starting their games. Time to see if you've learned anything."

"Yes, Chief." Mason swallowed, heart hammering.

The alarm bell shrieked, three rapid clangs, and the diving klaxon followed, a sound that drilled straight into the spine.

"Dive! Dive!"

The boat convulsed into action. Hatches slammed, vents opened, men lunged to stations. Mason flattened against the bulkhead as sailors charged past, shoulders brushing, boots hammering steel.

Main induction closed overhead with a hollow, final boom. *Pike* tilted nose-down, the deck sloping under Mason's feet. The air shifted instantly, damper, heavier, as water rushed into ballast tanks.

"Passing forty feet!"

Mason clutched a pipe, eyes fixed on the depth gauge as its needle swung. The hull groaned, a long, low complaint, but the men around him hardly blinked. Wheels spun, clipboards ticked, orders rattled like musket fire.

He forced himself to breathe in rhythm with the numbers called out. Passing forty-five feet... fifty... fifty-five... fifty-seven—scope coming up. At periscope depth, the diving officer raised a hand. "Level her. All stop."

The klaxon cut out. The silence after was deafening. Mason let his shoulders sag, realizing he had been holding his breath since the first clang.

"Not bad for a warm-up," Jensen said, appearing at his elbow with a grin.

O'Hara laughed. "Hell, that's just breakfast."

The next evolution sent *Pike* topside into the swell. Mason, roped into ammunition detail, clambered up behind the gun crew. The cold air slapped him, spray soaking his jumper in minutes. Ahead floated a rusted hulk, set as target practice.

"Load!"

Mason hauled a shell from the ready locker, surprised again by its weight. He passed it forward, arms burning as the gun crew slammed it home.

"Fire!"

The deck lurched with the recoil. The three-inch barked like thunder, and Mason's chest caught the shock. Smoke curled sharp in his nostrils, cordite burning his throat.

Out on the water, the hulk shuddered as steel tore into its flank.

"Good hit!" someone yelled.

Load, fire. Load, fire. The rhythm was brutal. Mason's muscles screamed, but he kept pace, teeth gritted. Each round's concussion rattled his bones, each blast a hammer on the sea itself.

When the cease-fire came, he leaned on the rail, gasping, clothes soaked with spray and sweat. His ears rang, and for the first time he noticed his own grin, wild and giddy.

"Not bad for a farm boy," O'Hara shouted, clapping his back hard enough to stagger him.

Mason could only laugh, breathless.

The destroyers came the next day, sleek gray hounds slicing through the swell, eager for blood.

"Contact bearing green one-zero, closing fast!"

Mason felt his pulse *spike* as the alarm sounded again. Men flew to stations, their voices taut, sharper than during drills.

"Dive! Dive!"

Pike plunged beneath the waves, bow angling steep. Mason relayed messages at a run, sweat slick despite the chill. "Engine room, hold steady on motors!" "Forward room, stand by to adjust trim!" His voice steadied with repetition, louder each time, as though speaking louder kept panic at bay.

The destroyer's propellers hammered overhead, a roar that vibrated through bone. Then came the depth charges, practice or not, they were real enough.

The hull jumped with each concussion, steel ringing like a bell. Dust shook from seams, gauges wobbled. Mason clung to the periscope well, heart pounding, eyes wide in the dim red light.

Another string went off closer. *Pike* shuddered, the air itself seeming to squeeze tight. A torpedoman across the control room muttered a prayer. Jensen grinned like a lunatic, lips pale, eyes fever-bright.

"Steady!" the diving officer barked. "Hold her level!"

The charges faded, the destroyer veering off. The sound of propellers receded, leaving the boat panting like a beast after a chase. Men exhaled all at once, nervous laughter bubbling up.

"Just a game," Jensen said, smirk returning. "Next time won't be."

Mason swallowed, nodding. He believed it.

They surfaced for bearings. Mason was in the passage with a clipboard when the klaxon shrieked again.

"Crash dive! Dive! Dive!"

He ran aft, shouting relays, as *Pike* tilted into her plunge. Hatches slammed, water hissed into ballast.

Then crack!

A flash burst from the control room panel. Sparks spat like angry hornets. The lights blinked out. For a heartbeat the boat was blind.

Smoke poured sharp and bitter. Men cursed, half-coughing.

Mason froze, terror rooting him. His mind screamed move! but his legs were stone.

"Smother it! Breaker three!" Nolan's voice cut through, sharp as an axe.

Mason dropped to his knees, yanked a rag from his pocket, and slapped it against the sparking wires. Heat seared his palm, but he pressed harder, choking the sparks. An electrician's mate slammed the breaker down, the snap echoing. The sparks died, the smoke thinning.

"Auxiliary lights on!"

Red bulbs flickered alive, painting the room bloody. Mason coughed, eyes stinging, but kept the rag pressed until the mate nodded and pulled it away.

"Good," Nolan said, hand clamping Mason's shoulder. "Didn't freeze. Remember that."

His legs shook, his chest burned, but he nodded. Around them, the crew reset, voices steady again. Orders rattled. The boat leveled at depth.

"Secure from casualty drill," the OOD called.

But Mason knew it hadn't been just a drill. The boat had bitten, testing them.

When the watch changed, Mason leaned against the bulkhead, sweat cold on his back, lungs still aching. His hands trembled, but no one jeered.

The electrician muttered, "Quick hands, kid." O'Hara thumped his arm. Jensen just grinned and said, "See? Even farm boys catch sparks."

It was the smallest things that mattered: not laughter at his expense, but acknowledgment. He had acted, not frozen.

Later, in his rack, Mason listened to *Pike*'s heartbeat, diesels hammering, water hissing in trim lines, the faint groan of hull against pressure. The sounds were familiar now, not foreign. The boat had tested him, and somehow, he had answered.

For the first time, he let sleep come without fighting it.

He didn't know how long he was out, only that Nolan's hand on his shoulder brought him back. "Up you get," the Chief murmured. "Skipper wants to see what she's made of."

The order came calm, clipped, as if the captain were asking for another cup of coffee. "Take her down to two-fifty. Down to two-fifty. After that, we find out her breaking point."

Mason's throat went dry. Nolan leaned close, voice low. "Every boat gets taken down, messman. Steel's got to prove itself. So do we."

Ballast hissed. The bow dipped. The depth gauge needle crept: one hundred... one-fifty... two hundred. The hull answered with a groan, deep and pained. Rivets pinged like gunshots in the dark.

"Two-fifty feet," the planesman reported.

"Hold her steady."

They did. The control room went still, save for the sound of the sea pressing. Sweat traced down faces, though the air was cool. Mason gripped his clipboard until his knuckles whitened, eyes fixed on the gauge.

"Another thirty feet," the captain ordered.

The gauge dropped again.

"Two-seventy."

The hull sang, a low animal sound that made Mason's bones ache.

"Two-eighty."

The control room was all heartbeats and creaks.

"Two-ninety."

Then the hiss came, thin and sharp, from the after torpedo room.

"Flooding aft! Flooding in the after room!"

The word flooding tore through the boat like a round through flesh. Spray shrieked against steel, seawater hammering through a failed packing gland. The smell followed, raw, unmistakable, the ocean inside where it had no right to be.

"Level her!" the captain barked. "Stand by to blow main ballast, roof vents!"

At that depth there was no half measure. Once you blew main ballast, you were going for a ride whether you liked it or not. The air would expand as the boat rose, and the submarine would ride it like a bullet in a barrel.

"Blow main! Brace!"

Compressed air roared through *Pike*'s belly. The bow kicked, and the boat pitched upward like a bucking horse. Mason slammed into the bulkhead as the deck tilted to a 20-degree up-angle. Tools clattered aft like loose shot. Coffee tins skidded, wrenches flew. Men who weren't braced slid into each other, swearing.

"Angle twenty! Rising fast!" the diving officer shouted.

Water from the aft leak surged aft with the tilt, sluicing across decks and into cable runs. The smell of ozone cut through seawater a heartbeat before it happened.

"Short circuit aft!" someone screamed. A panel spat sparks, white and furious, lighting the red gloom with flares. An electrician threw himself onto the breaker, locking it down with both hands as arcs snapped around him.

Mason scrambled aft, repeating Nolan's order: "One man stays on the breaker, don't leave it! Dog the inner door if you have to!"

The leak crew fought like men in a storm cellar. Spray lashed the compartment like a whip. A pry bar wedged into the valve wheel; Mason shoved his shoulder into the bar with two others, teeth clenched until the wheel grudged over. The spray faltered, then slowed, the hiss dying by degrees.

"Leak contained!" a soaked torpedoman roared.

The ascent didn't wait for them. *Pike* shot upward, her bow knifing for daylight. Mason's stomach lurched as the deck shuddered underfoot. They were passengers now, riding the boat's desperate exhale.

"Passing one hundred, eighty feet!" the planesman yelled, voice breaking with the strain.

Then came the breach.

The bow slammed into the surface, shouldering green water aside in a geyser. For an instant *Pike* broke free, weightless, the ocean gone from under her. Mason's stomach rose, his boots floating off steel, every man aboard caught in a moment of impossible suspension.

Then gravity came back. The hull crashed down into the sea with a bone-deep slam, throwing men into bulkheads, rattling teeth and ribs. The whole boat groaned like a wounded beast settling on its haunches.

Silence. Just water running off steel, men panting, coffee dripping where it had splattered on the overhead.

"Surface," the OOD reported, voice shaking.

"Secure main blow," the captain said evenly, though his knuckles were white on the chart table. "All compartments report."

"Aft flooding contained. Electrical bus isolated."

"Forward all secure."

"Control secure."

One by one the reports came, voices hoarse but steady.

The captain nodded once. "Very well. OOD set course for Mare Island."

The mess was alive with men trying to laugh off fear, each in his own way. Shirts clung wet with spray and sweat, faces pale and eyes too bright, but no one wanted to admit it.

"Three hundred feet." Jensen's voice carried, soft but insistent, as though naming it out loud gave it weight. "By God, we touched it."

"Touched it, rode it, and got spat out like Jonah," O'Hara muttered, rubbing a bruise blooming on his temple. "Never thought I'd feel my boots float in a submarine."

"You weren't floating," the torpedoman second class snorted. "You were sprawled across me. Get off next time."

That cracked the compartment, laughter spilling too hard, too fast, like a valve opened against too much pressure. It wasn't funny, not really, but it was laughter or the shakes. Mason laughed with them, voice high, shaky, but real.

At the end of the table Mac shoved coffee cups around like lifelines. "Drink, or I'll pour it down your throats myself." He didn't insult anyone this time; the cook knew when to jab and when to feed.

The electrician's mate who'd held the breaker sat silent, a cigarette trembling between his fingers. When Mason passed him the sugar, he finally spoke: "Panel should've gone. Should've burned us all. I don't know why it didn't."

"Because you were sitting on the breaker like Saint Peter at the gate," Jensen said, trying for humor. "Nobody gets through unless you say so."

The electrician's mouth twitched. "Saint Peter doesn't get soaked with bilge water, Jensen."

"No, but I bet he smells like it," O'Hara shot back. More laughter, weaker this time, but steadier.

Mason nursed his coffee, still tasting salt in his throat. He could hear the memory of the leak, the shriek of water at pressure, the animal groan of steel. He'd been sure they were gone, yet here they sat, alive, joking, bruised but breathing.

Across from him Nolan smoked in silence, then finally spoke, quiet but certain. "We proved her. She'll take two-fifty without complaint, more if she has to. That's what you came away with." He tapped ash into a tin lid. "What you don't write in a report is what keeps you alive."

The captain, passing through, overheard. He paused, eyes scanning the tired, wet faces, then said evenly, "Today was a training exercise. Nothing more. The record will reflect a routine dive."

"Aye, sir," came the chorus, automatic. But Mason saw the looks that passed between the men. Every one of them knew the truth: *Pike* had gone deep, touched the edge, and come back fighting. That would never make ink on a page, but it would live in every man's bones.

Later, in the racks, Jensen whispered across the dark. "Farm boy. You felt it too, didn't you? Not the water, the boat. She wanted out."

"Yeah," Mason whispered back. "I felt it."

"Good," Jensen said, and rolled over, the grin audible in his voice.

Mason lay awake a while longer, hand pressed to the steel by his shoulder, listening to *Pike* hum her weary tune. They had asked her for her limit. She'd screamed at them, slapped them, and then carried them home.

No report would show it. But Mason knew, and now, he belonged.

Chapter 7
The Boat Breathes

The coast came up gray and cold, the Pacific rolling heavy under a low lid of clouds. *Pike* limped south, engines steady but subdued, her hull sweating rust where the paint had burned from the test dive. The men were quieter than usual. Even the galley noise had dropped to half volume. They were listening, to the boat, to themselves, to the fact they were still breathing.

From the bridge Mason could smell land before he saw it: wet earth, distant smoke, a sweetness that didn't belong to salt water. After weeks of diesel, sweat, and fear, that smell alone felt like permission to be human again.

"Point Reyes off the starboard bow," the quartermaster called.

Nolan leaned on the coaming beside Mason. "There she is. First smell of home always hits harder after you think you've lost it."

"You think the captain's going to tell them what happened?" Mason asked.

"Not a chance. We had a drill, we handled it, we came home. That's the story." Nolan gave a half-smile that didn't reach his eyes. "But she'll remember. So will we."

Fog thickened as they entered the bay. The whistle moaned once, long and low, and the echo bounced off unseen hills. Sounded like the ocean sighing relief. The pilot boat came out of the mist, a squat, black-hulled thing throwing spray, and the pilot climbed aboard with a practiced hop, cap pulled down against drizzle.

"Morning, gentlemen," he said cheerfully. "You brought the weather with you, I see."

"Better than bringing the bottom," Nolan muttered.

By late morning the cranes of Mare Island slid into view, angular and black against the clouds. Yard tugs were already waiting, their decks slick with rain. The air smelled of river mud and paint thinner; gulls circled and screamed. The dockside looked like a battlefield fought with wrenches instead of guns, sparks arcing, steam venting, men shouting over compressors.

"Lines over!" The captain's voice carried sharp and clear. Ropes hissed through wet chocks. When the first line caught a bollard, the boat shuddered to stillness. For the first time in weeks, *Pike* stopped moving.

Engines died. The sudden quiet felt wrong, as if the world had forgotten to breathe. Then the creak of dock timbers and the distant clang of a hammer filled the void, and the crew remembered how to move again.

Mason stayed topside as long as he could. Watching the tugs pull away, he felt a strange ache, like leaving something unfinished. Nolan came up beside him, hands buried in his peacoat.

"Don't look so lost, kid. She'll wait for us. Boats always do."

"I just never realized how much noise land makes," Mason said. "Feels like everything's shouting."

"That's industry," Nolan said dryly. "God's way of reminding sailors we're replaceable."

The gangway clanged down, and the yard came aboard like a boarding party. Men in gray coveralls with clipboards and pocket wrenches moved through compartments that still smelled of sweat and bilge. One of them tapped the pressure hull with a hammer and called out numbers to another scribbling on a pad.

Mason followed them for a while, uneasy. Watching strangers pry into the *Pike* felt indecent, like letting someone read your letters. A welder marked a weld seam near the after room, and the chalk squealed on steel.

"Don't mind the noise," the man said without looking up. "We're just seeing what held and what didn't."

"She held," Mason said before he could stop himself.

The welder glanced up, a little smile in his soot-streaked

face. "Yeah, I figured that. Otherwise you wouldn't be here arguing with me."

Below, Nolan guided the electricians through a controlled shutdown. The air compressors sighed, the battery blowers wound down, and the big switchboard went dark. For the first time since commissioning, the boat had no heartbeat of her own.

"Feels like she's sleeping," Mason said quietly.

"Don't get sentimental," Nolan answered, though his hand lingered on the bulkhead. "Sleep's how she heals."

By afternoon the captain, XO, and a pair of yard officers toured the damage. Mason caught a glimpse of them through the open hatch to Control, four men moving in a tight cluster, murmuring in low, official voices.

The XO pointed to the logbook. "Note: minor electrical fault during training dive. Corrective action taken. Recommend inspection of aft packing prior to next operation."

The captain initialed it, pen scratching softly. "That'll do."

The yard officer nodded. "Routine then."

"Routine," the captain repeated.

Mason felt Nolan's hand on his shoulder. "That's how the Navy keeps its pride polished, son. Routine saves paperwork."

"Doesn't feel routine."

"Good. Means you learned something."

They were billeted in a row of temporary barracks near the river, thin-walled, smelling of damp wood and soap powder. The bunks didn't sway, which should have been a blessing. But Mason woke every hour, heart jumping at the phantom creak of nonexistent hull plates. By dawn he gave up and stepped outside.

The yard was already alive, steam drifting from manholes, hammering echoing off the cranes. Across the water, San Pablo Bay glimmered under a lid of gray cloud. The air tasted of rust and rain. Somewhere a siren blew to start another shift, and Mason felt suddenly out of step with the world. On patrol, the day belonged to the boat. Here it belonged to clocks.

O'Hara came out behind him, rubbing his eyes. "Can't sleep?"

"Nope."

"None of us can. Deck don't move right."

They stood there a while, watching the cranes swing like lazy metronomes.

"Bet the captain sleeps fine," O'Hara said.

"That's because he's got a conscience made of steel," Mason said, half-smiling.

"Nah. He just drinks better whiskey."

The next few days blurred. Mason joined the work parties without needing orders. He carried paint tins, fetched gaskets, crawled into bilges with a rag and a flashlight. The smells of acetone, hot metal, and new insulation filled the boat. Sparks rained from welders like orange snow. When the yard crew re-sealed the aft packing, Nolan supervised every turn of the wrench.

"Again," Nolan said, voice calm but absolute. "Until I say it's tight."

The fitter gave the wrench another quarter-turn. The gland groaned faintly.

"Now it's tight," Nolan said.

The fitter leaned back, grinning. "You're a hard man to please, Chief."

"That's why we're all still breathing."

By evening the compartment glowed faintly with the sheen of new metal. Mason ran a rag along the bulkhead and caught his own reflection in the polished surface. For a second he saw someone older looking back.

The shipyard had a rhythm all its own, a kind of metallic heartbeat that thudded through the air from dawn to dusk. Hammers struck steel with the same tempo as pistons, grinders whined, and the smell of hot paint, oil, and saltwater mixed into something only a sailor could love.

Pike lay between two destroyers at a mud-brown pier, her decks draped in cables and hoses. Her hatches were propped open like the mouths of sleeping animals. Yard crews swarmed aboard, coveralls streaked in primer and graphite, voices clipped and confident. To them, *Pike* was just another hull number, one more job before payday. To her crew, she was still the boat that had clawed its way up from 300 feet and lived to tell it.

Mason joined the work parties early. He couldn't stand still long enough to let someone else touch his boat without helping. He hauled power leads, fetched tools, and polished brass until his hands smelled of metal. Sometimes he stopped to listen, not for men, but for the faint, hollow ring of the hull being tested by the yard's hammers. It was a different kind of heartbeat now, slow and steady, like someone recovering from a fever.

Nolan moved through it all like a man checking a sleeping child, quiet, thorough, occasionally fierce. "Don't let 'em rush the aft seal," he warned Mason. "Yard'll say it's good enough if it doesn't drip. I want it better than good."

"Yes, Chief."

The burned panel aft was next. The electrician's mate, the same one who had ridden the breaker through the short, stood beside a civilian tech while they stripped and re-insulated the wires. The tech hummed an off-key tune. The mate didn't speak until Mason brought him coffee.

"She almost lit up like a Christmas tree," the mate said quietly. "You don't forget the smell of burning insulation at that angle. It's... sweet, like candy gone bad."

Mason nodded. "You did good."

"Good ain't what kept us alive," the mate said, tapping the panel. "Luck did. And maybe her." He thumped the hull once, as if acknowledging *Pike* herself.

Afternoons bled into evenings. The yard crew left at whistle; *Pike*'s men stayed. They coiled lines, cleaned bilges, painted anything that didn't move, and checked what the yard left undone. Every clang from a hammer made someone flinch the first few days, but by the week's end, the sounds blended into background, just another kind of ocean.

At night, the men were billeted in wooden barracks that smelled of dust and weak coffee. The beds didn't sway, which should have been a blessing. But the stillness woke them. O'Hara snored like an air compressor. Jensen dreamt loud, mumbling commands and curses. Mason rolled over again and again, half expecting the floor to tilt under him.

When dawn came, he was already up. The morning fog hugged the ground, muffling sound. He walked to the pier and watched the yard men uncover the boat for work. The cranes were already creaking, cables swaying overhead like giant spider legs. *Pike* looked tired but defiant, her paint patched, her scars showing faintly under primer.

"You look like you've been out here a while," Nolan said behind him, a steaming cup in hand.

"Couldn't sleep."

"Good. Means you're part of her now."

Mason half smiled. "Is that the secret?"

"The secret," Nolan said, "is knowing you don't own the boat. She owns you."

By midweek, the Navy inspectors arrived, clipboards, sharp pencils, no humor. They moved compartment by compartment, checking pressure gauges, hull readings, logbooks. One lieutenant, clean-shaven and far too polite, asked Nolan if the "training exercise" had caused any unusual stress on the hull.

"None worth mentioning," Nolan said evenly. "She's as sound as when we left San Diego."

The lieutenant nodded, satisfied. He didn't notice the flicker of eyes that passed between the crew, the silent agreement that what happened below 250 feet would never hit paper.

When the officers left, Jensen muttered, "Guess that's that. We didn't almost drown. We just trained real hard."

"Exactly," O'Hara said. "You ever notice the Navy's good at forgettin' the stuff that makes her nervous?"

Mac barked from the galley truck, "Shut your traps and eat. Food's better when you chew instead of talk."

The first liberty after the inspection felt like parole. Vallejo's bars filled fast, a tide of khaki, laughter, and cheap perfume. Jukeboxes rattled with brass and drums, the kind of music that made a man forget he'd nearly died a week ago. Mason stuck close to Jensen, O'Hara, and Nolan. It wasn't so much loyalty as gravity; you stayed with the ones who'd seen you scared.

They ended up in a narrow tavern near the ferry dock, the kind of place that smelled of whiskey and waxed floors.

The bartender barely looked up, he'd seen submariners before.

"To *Pike*," Jensen said, raising his glass. "May she never spring another leak."

"Or if she does," O'Hara added, "may I not be the one nearest the valve."

Laughter followed, loud enough to draw stares. They didn't care. You earned laughter the hard way.

Nolan didn't toast. He just sipped, his expression unreadable. After a while he said, "Boats don't hold grudges. But they remember who listened."

Mason thought of the yard fitter's words. "Funny. Somebody told me the same thing this morning."

"Then maybe you're starting to hear right," Nolan said.

They left the bar late, walking the riverfront. The fog was rolling in, soft and low, muting the streetlamps. Across the channel, the cranes at Mare Island were haloed in mist, their lights glowing like stars.

O'Hara tilted his head back and whistled. "Never thought I'd say it, but she looks almost pretty from here."

"She's resting," Nolan said.

"She's waiting," Mason corrected.

The last inspection came on a gray morning two weeks later. The captain, XO, and yard superintendent stood by the gangway trading quiet words. The superintendent's clipboard held a neat summary: Routine refit completed.

Pressure test satisfactory. Training dive results within expectations.

No one said 300 feet. No one would.

The captain signed the form, shook the man's hand, and turned to the crew. "We're cleared to sail. We'll run light drills on the way down the coast. Let's show the yard what a real boat sounds like."

A cheer went up, not loud, but full. The kind that starts in the chest and ends with a grin you can't hide.

By noon, *Pike*'s hatches were closed again. The new paint gleamed, the scars hidden. The dock gang pulled shore power, and the familiar hum of the batteries came alive. The engines coughed, then settled into that steady rhythm every submariner knows, a heartbeat you could trust.

Nolan walked through each compartment one last time, palm brushing steel, listening. "Quieter," he murmured. "She's ready."

Mason stood topside as the lines were singled up. Mare Island stretched out behind him, cranes black against a sky washed pale by fog. The smell of river and oil filled his lungs, and for the first time he realized he loved it.

"Lines clear," came the call.

"Cast off all."

The captain raised a hand, and *Pike* eased from the pier, her wake curling through brown water. The tugs gave her a gentle shove into the channel. The men on deck stood a little straighter. They weren't passengers now; they were crew again.

Nolan stepped up beside Mason. "Feels right, doesn't it?"

"Yeah," Mason said. "Like she's breathing again."

"She is," Nolan said. "And so are we."

The afternoon sun began breaking through as they cleared the bay's narrower reaches. The tug dropped its line and peeled away with a blast of its horn. The pilot stayed aboard, cap low, eyes on the tide. "Slack water in half an hour," he said. "We'll ride the ebb right under the Gate."

Mason looked ahead, toward the faint outline of the Golden Gate Bridge rising out of the haze. The light was shifting gold now, the bay turning the color of brass. The Pacific waited beyond, blue and endless. He grinned despite himself.

"Underway again," he said quietly.

"Underway again," Nolan echoed. "Let's see what else she's got to say."

They mustered early for sea, the yard men stepping back as *Pike*'s crew slipped lines back into their own hands. Mare Island's cranes stood against a sky rinsed clean by a weak wind; gulls tilted like lazy paper planes. The captain's last word at the pier was plain as water: "We'll log our drills as drills. We'll remember the rest ourselves."

The pilot clomped aboard with a wool cap and a short pencil. "We'll ride the slack, catch the start of the ebb," he said to the OOD. "Carquinez will be a little squirrely, crosswind down San Pablo, then it opens. You boys mind your tug and I'll mind the channel."

"Copy," the OOD said, the word meaning we've done hard things; we can do this too.

"Single up," came the order. Lines dropped to singles, winch drums muttering. "Cast off bow. Cast off stern." The last spring line went light, and *Pike* eased free of the pier as if she had been holding her breath and could finally let it go. The tug took a lazy strain and pointed her nose downriver. Men on the pier watched and waved because that's what men do when other men go somewhere they can't see from shore.

Mason stood topside with a lanyard clipped and the river's brown smell in his nose. Mare Island slid astern, cranes becoming toys, welders' sparks fireflies in daylight. Nolan came up, hands in pockets, the set of him lighter than it had been in a week.

"Been awhile since we went under way without someone else's tools on our back," he said.

"Feels like we've got our skin back," Mason answered.

They threaded the Napa River into Carquinez Strait, the hills on either side close and green, the water running two colors where currents argued. The tug skipper waved, kicked his boat's stern aside, and set *Pike* to her own engines. The diesels rumbled up, alive, even, content. The vibration came through the deck into Mason's boots like a dog leaning against your knees.

Vallejo fell away with its wharfside bars and laughter they could almost still hear. Then the strait widened into San Pablo Bay, a shallow sheet of sun-shot chop. The afternoon light softened and went to yellow. The pilot squinted at the marks and pointed with his whole arm. "Buoy left. Give that mudflats room. You'll eat bottom if you get cocky."

They didn't. They followed his finger and the black line on the chart and the deeper line every man aboard could feel in his bones: the way out.

Richmond's tanks gleamed to starboard, a white forest. Mount Tam rose to port in blue folds. Then Marin opened its gate to San Francisco Bay, and the city announced itself with a skyline that still found ways to surprise sailors who'd seen it a dozen times. The Ferry Building clock put its hands where late afternoon ought to be. Streetcars stitched the waterfront. Shore patrols turned their caps to the wind.

"Pilot, we'll take it from here on your mark," the OOD said.

"You'll want me through the slot," the pilot said dryly. "But if you insist, I'll tell you when to throw me back."

They laughed, only a little tense. The current took a new bite as the tide turned, just enough to set the bow to starboard if you let it. They didn't.

And then the bridge.

The Golden Gate lifted out of haze like a red wire strung between two granite fists. It was both bigger and finer than men remembered: a piece of engineering so audacious even sailors shut up for a minute to look. Sun leaned west, the cables taking it and throwing it down in long bars of copper light across the water. The ocean beyond was a deep plate of hammered blue. The wind right there at the throat was colder, saltier, honest.

"Make a note, Quartermaster," the captain said softly. "Passing under Golden Gate, outbound."

"Aye, sir," the QM said, neat as a pin, pencil sure.

Mason swallowed without meaning to. The red steel above felt like a gate you passed through in a church, the kind that divided the part of the service you remembered from the part that changed you.

"Clip tight," Nolan said at his shoulder, but his voice had lost its edge. "And look. You want to remember this as a picture, not a rumor."

They passed under. The bridge's underworks rattled and hummed with car tires and wind. Shadows ran down *Pike*'s deck in stripes and then were gone; sun hit her in a broad, forgiving sheet. Ahead, the Pacific lay out like a table set for a long meal, place cards written in swells and white lines of wind. Far out, evening built itself, gold giving to orange, to a bruised purple at the rim.

The pilot tipped his cap. "You won't need me now."

"Thank you," the captain said. "We'll put you ashore."

The pilot's launch came alongside, clean, quick, and took him back to his world of buoys and tides and men who followed them. *Pike* kept her heading west for a hundred heartbeats longer than she needed to, as if to test the size of what waited, then took her southing on orders that felt like a promise kept.

"Rig for sea," the XO called. "Set watches as posted."

"Aye."

Below, control took on its sea-face: clips checked, tags checked, men checked each other because that's how you catch the one thing you didn't see yourself. The after room, clean, tight, newly shy about bragging, smelled faintly of fresh paint and memory. The panel aft hummed as if to say we're fine, we're fine, hush.

On the bridge, wind took caps and tempers and smoothed them both. O'Hara leaned on the coaming and tried not to look like he was leaning. Jensen hummed half a tune that wasn't the one on any jukebox. The sun slid to the exact place where the sea holds it without dropping, then, with a little theatricality, let it go.

"Pretty," Mason said, before he could stop himself.

"Honest," Nolan corrected, not unkind. "Pretty lies. Honest keeps you alive."

They stood and watched until the edge swallowed the last gold. Then the captain's voice came up the voicepipe with the calm authority of a man who had decided to trust both steel and the men inside it.

"Take her down to one-fifty."

"Diving, aye," came the reply. The horn brayed once, men

sealed the little world, and *Pike* slipped beneath the skin as lightly as a thought that you mean to hold on to.

San Francisco dimmed behind them; Mare Island was already a story they'd tell with hands and coffee cups. Water pressed. Steel answered. Inside, men found their places by hand without looking. Mason set his boots where the deck told him to and felt, unmistakably, that the boat's breath and his were finally the same length.

Outbound, under the bridge, with the sun falling into the west, *Pike* was back at sea.

Chapter 8
Shakedown South

The water closed above them with a smooth hiss. The last golden rays of sunset filtered down in pale shafts through the periscope shears, then faded to green shadow. *Pike* was alone again, suspended in that half-lit world between surface and sea floor, moving south at ten knots.

"Passing one-five-zero feet," the diving officer reported.

"Hold her there," the captain replied, voice steady. "Engines ahead one-third. Let's see how she feels after her yard work."

Mason stood near the aft bulkhead, the thrum of the motors steady under his boots. The light in Control was dim and red, the air heavy with oil and sweat. He could hear everything: the faint squeal of the depth gauge needle, the whisper of trim pumps, the muted click of a valve handle turning somewhere forward. The sounds were familiar now, not frightening, not strange. Just alive.

"Feels good," Nolan murmured beside him. "Tight again. You can tell when she's right by the way the hull talks. Listen."

Mason did. The steel creaked softly, like an old house breathing in its sleep. He nodded.

Nolan grinned faintly. "Aye. She's telling us she's glad to be back."

They ran deep for an hour, then rose to periscope depth. The sea above had gone black, broken only by a few scattered reflections of starlight. The Pacific was calm, almost eerily so. The captain scanned the horizon, then lowered the scope.

"Nothing but water and stars," he said. "Let's run submerged to dawn."

Engines shifted to battery. The hum changed pitch; the air grew stiller, heavier. Men spoke softer now, their voices absorbed by the sea pressing all around them. Mason made rounds with Nolan, checking gauges, feeling for heat on bearings, listening to the new cables hum faintly in their trays. The boat's systems, her "nerves," as Nolan called them, were working like they should.

"Good work aft," Nolan said, glancing at the log. "We'll keep her that way. Tomorrow, we'll give her teeth a test."

At dawn, *Pike* came to the surface off Monterey Bay. A long, gentle swell rocked her hull, gulls circling low overhead. The air was cold and clean, scented faintly of pine from the coast. The crew blinked in the sunlight, pale, blinking men coming back to the world.

"Engines ahead two-thirds," the captain ordered from the bridge. "We'll stay surfaced until Point Conception."

Mason climbed up for topside watch. The deck was slick with dew, the steel cold under his hands. The wind off the bow smelled of salt and diesel exhaust, the perfume of a working boat. He looked aft at the feather of white wake trailing behind *Pike* and felt something stir in his chest. This was no longer terror. This was belonging.

Nolan appeared through the hatch with a cup of coffee, handing it up without a word.

"Thanks, Chief."

"Don't thank me. You'll spill half of it anyway."

Mason grinned. "Not if I drink it fast."

"Then you'll burn your tongue. Either way, you lose."

They shared a quiet moment, the kind submariners treasure, the world reduced to sky, horizon, and the sound of the diesels pounding steady beneath them.

"You ever get used to it?" Mason asked.

"To what?"

"This. Just... being out here. The noise, the smell, the waiting."

Nolan took a sip, eyes on the horizon. "You don't get used to it. You get tuned to it. Like a machine that finally runs smooth. Once that happens, everything else on land feels wrong."

Mason nodded slowly. "Yeah. It already does."

By noon they were sixty miles south, the coast a thin brown smudge on the horizon. The captain called for drills.

"All hands, prepare for maneuvering trials. Let's see if the yard left us anything loose."

The next two hours were a blur of angles and orders: ten-degree down bubble, then up; engines ahead full, then stop; rudder hard right, then steady on course. *Pike* rolled and dipped like a living thing, shaking off her stiffness. Tools clattered faintly in the engine room, coffee cups skittered across tables, but everything held. No leaks, no alarms, no shorted circuits.

When they leveled off again, the captain nodded toward Nolan. "Chief, that's a fine tune you gave her."

Nolan just said, "Aye, sir," but Mason could see the pride in the man's eyes.

Later, during a battery charge topside, Mason caught Nolan leaning on the fairwater rail, squinting toward the horizon.

"She's right again," Nolan said. "Good boat. Good men. Don't take much more than that."

Mason nodded. "Feels like we can do anything."

Nolan gave a quiet chuckle. "That's the feeling that gets men killed. Keep the respect, lose the fear, but never forget either."

By mid-afternoon the next day they reached the waters off Point Conception, where the Navy often ran fleet exercises. A destroyer silhouette waited in the distance, USS *Stewart*, one of the old four-stackers serving as a torpedo target ship for training.

"Sound that contact," the captain ordered.

"Single screw, fast, bearing two-one-zero," the sound man replied, voice clipped. "Range about six thousand yards and closing."

The XO leaned over the chart. "Let's give him something to chase. Helm, come left twenty degrees. Periscope depth."

"Aye, sir."

Mason felt the shift as the planes bit water and the boat angled down. The lights dimmed; the sea closed over them again. At forty feet, the captain called, "All stop. Let's get quiet."

The destroyer's screws drummed faintly through the hull, fast, deliberate, like a predator that knew it wasn't hunting for real. This was practice, but the crew treated it like combat. They'd all heard the stories of practice runs gone wrong.

"Prepare tubes one and two," the captain ordered. "Exercise heads only."

Forward, the torpedomen readied the fish, their hands quick and practiced. Valves opened with metallic sighs.

Pressure built in the tubes. Mason checked the trim readings, solid.

"Bearing... steady," the XO murmured. "Angle on the bow, thirty port. Range four thousand and closing."

"Match bearings and shoot," the captain said quietly.

"Tube one, fire!"

The boat shuddered faintly. A heartbeat later, "Tube two, fire!"

Compressed air whooshed, then silence. Every man counted under his breath.

"Impact... now," Jensen whispered.

Nothing, then the sonar man smiled. "Target ping, two hits, sir."

A ripple of quiet pride spread through the control room. Not cheering, just the quiet satisfaction of professionals doing their job.

"Secure tubes one and two," the captain ordered. "Well done, gentlemen. We'll log it clean."

Nolan leaned toward Mason. "Not bad for a bunch of yard monkeys."

Mason grinned. "She shoots straight, Chief."

"She does if we load her right. Remember that."

The sun dipped low as they ran surfaced along the Santa Barbara Channel. The sea had gone glassy again, reflecting the sky in long golden streaks. The captain allowed the bridge watch to stay topside; even he seemed reluctant to go below.

For the first time since the test dive off Oregon, the laughter on deck came easy. Mac leaned out of the hatch with coffee mugs, sloshing but grinning. Jensen sat on the gun deck, cleaning a shell case that hadn't been fired yet, humming some tune that didn't belong to any radio. O'Hara stood beside Mason at the rail, watching dolphins ride the bow wave.

"They follow us every time," O'Hara said. "Maybe they think we're one of them."

"Maybe we are," Mason said.

The water hissed past the hull, rhythmic, alive. The boat felt different now, lighter, surer, almost eager. She'd been tested, bruised, patched, and reborn. The men aboard her had been too.

Nolan came topside, hands in his jacket pockets. "Enjoy it while it lasts, boys. Tomorrow we see what the gun can do."

"More drills, Chief?" Jensen groaned.

Nolan smiled faintly. "Always. You keep practicing until it's boring, then one day it stops being practice."

Mason nodded. "And that's when the real thing starts."

"Aye," Nolan said quietly. "And none of us will need to ask what to do."

That night, as Pike cruised on the surface under a sky full of stars, Mason stood his watch on the fairwater. The diesels thundered below, the wind cool on his face. The lights of the coast blinked faintly to port, small, fragile things in a big, dark world.

For the first time, he didn't feel small himself. The ocean no longer frightened him. The boat didn't just carry him; it trusted him to be part of her.

Nolan's voice echoed faintly from below, calling for the next watch section. Mason smiled, adjusting his cap against the wind.

Tomorrow, torpedoes. Then the gun. Then San Diego, and whatever waits beyond.

He looked forward along the dark deck, the horizon fading into black water, and felt the hum of the diesels deep in his chest, the heartbeat of something alive, steady, and proud.

They slid past dawn with glassy seas and a breeze that smelled faintly of sage rolling off the coast. By midmorning the quartermaster had Point Mugu off the bow and a set of rendezvous marks penciled on the chart. A faint mast pricked the southern horizon, target tug with a canvas drogue astern, and farther east a skinny destroyer profile kept station, bored and watchful. The Pacific had that big empty look men mistake for kindness.

"Clear the bridge," the captain said, voice carrying clean in the sunshine. "We'll go under for the first run."

Hatches clanged. The horn gave its single solemn note.

"Dive, dive!"

Air thundered out of ballast. The bow dipped and the ocean took them, green, then dim, then the close, familiar red of Control. It felt like closing a door on noise. The world narrowed to steel and purpose.

"Passing fifty feet."

"Make your depth four-five. Periscope depth."

Mason took his spot by the periscope well with Nolan just off his shoulder. Forward, the torpedo room thudded to life: valves cracking, pumps starting, voices tight with focus. The sound man sang bearings like fiddle notes, target tug slow and steady, destroyer meandering wide on the quarter like a sheepdog killing time.

"Prepare tubes one and two," the captain said. "Exercise heads. Flood both."

"Tube room, flood one and two, flooding," came back, the mate's voice flat with drill-calm. "Pressures rising... equalized."

The XO leaned over the plot with his pencil, the quartermaster sliding the maneuvering board under his hand. "Gyro three-six-five," he murmured. "Angle on the bow twenty port. Bearing steady, range twenty-eight hundred, decreasing."

"Match bearings and shoot," the captain said softly.

"Open outer doors one and two."

"Outer doors open."

Mason felt his jaw tense against the quiet. You never heard the important part. Only the breath around it, the minute flex of steel, the way the floor seemed to shrug when a fish went out. He thought about the first time he'd watched this, how noise had been fear back then. Now the hush felt like competence.

"Tube one, FIRE."

A pause in the boat's pulse, then the smallest kick through the hull. Somewhere forward a man said, "One away."

"Tube two, FIRE."

"Two away."

The sound man tracked the tug's small engine, the drag of the drogue, the soft doubling the exercise head made when it thumped the sled. He lifted one finger, then two. "Good echoes. Two hits, sir."

No one cheered. Breath went out, breath came back, men looked at their hands and found they weren't shaking. The captain nodded once. "Very well. Secure tubes one and two. Flood three and four, second run, destroyer guard in close."

"Guard's turning in," the sound man warned, voice tightening. "Bearing two-two-five, range three thousand and moving."

The XO's pencil flicked changes like a metronome tick. "Gyro three-five-seven. Range twenty-two hundred. Angle on the bow now fifteen port, he's tightening his circle."

The captain lowered the periscope, face a mask. "We'll take the shot through his screen. Helm, come right three degrees. Hold periscope depth."

"Aye."

Mason relayed without being told; the words felt right in his mouth now. "Forward room, stand by three and four. Outer doors stay shut until I call."

"Standing by."

Nolan touched the periscope column with three fingers, habit, superstition, test. "You feel that?"

Mason didn't answer at first, listening with his knees more than his ears. "Swell's got a longer leg. We'll get the scope drunk if we rush it."

"Good," Nolan said. "Now say it to the man who needs to hear it."

Mason leaned toward the diving officer. "Scope's getting slop, sir."

The DO cut his eyes to the bubble, then to the captain. "Recommend a count before each look. Swell's long."

The captain grunted assent. "Up scope." He waited a beat through the roll, took his quick slice, then "Down." "Match and shoot."

"Open outer doors three and four," the XO called.

"Outer doors open."

"Three, FIRE."

"Four, FIRE."

The destroyer's screw-threads thrummed closer, then swung away; practice is practice, but even in drills the guard captain didn't feel inclined to eat an exercise head. The sound man smiled without showing teeth. "Two thumps on the sled. Guard's still playing dog. No booms." A ripple of amusement ran through the room and died of its own accord.

"Secure from firing," the captain said. "Prepare to surface. Tug will want his toys back."

They blew the tanks with a civilized sigh and came up into nine inches of breeze and a long, bright swell. The target tug trundled in to haul the floating exercise heads by their lifting eyes, the little boat's winch whining. The destroyer leaned in to pass a signal with flags, GOOD RUN STOP NEXT RUN SURFACE, then peeled off, bored again.

"Up we go," the captain said. "Let the gun crew wake their pet."

They manned the three-inch like old friends meeting at a bar. Gun captain at the breech, pointer and trainer on their wheels, loader crouched low, second loader at the ready box, a phone talker with a handset pressed to one ear and a string of "aye"s ready for the wind. The target was a battered buoy sluiced with old splinters and big as a barge door, hard to miss and somehow always missed by the overconfident.

"Load HE," the gun captain barked. "Short fuses. We're splashing, not fishing."

"Load," the loader echoed, sliding the round up and home. The brass case kissed the chamber with a sound Mason could have picked out of a choir. "Up!"

"Stand by!" The OOD's voice came over the bridge speaker, crisp on salt air. "Fire when you bear. Watch your roll."

The boat had a lazy starboard sway. The trainer called it under his breath, back... back... back, then, "On!" The pointer had his sight settled, the gun captain watching the nose of the swell like a boxer reads a shoulder.

"Fire!"

The gun barked, the deck hopped. Smoke curled up and back, whip-lashed by wind. A white splash bloomed short and right, the sea swallowing it with polite indifference.

"Short by twenty!" the spotter yelled, eyes behind binoculars.

"Up five, right two," the gun captain snapped. "Load!"

Brass clanged. "Up!"

"Fire!"

This time the splash leapt across the target's face. Closer. Mason felt the grin trying to climb his face and shoved it down, helping the second loader pull the next round from the ready box, feeling the weight, the solid promise of it in gloved hands.

The third shot shattered a rusted hoop on the buoy and set a gull to swearing. The gun crew whooped once, quickly, and got back to work. A fourth round hit clean, center of ugly, and the buoy lurched on its chain like a hung man taking one last offense.

"Cease," the OOD called. "Well enough. We're not painting a picture."

Brass lay like gold on the deck. Mason and Jensen scrambled to police it, the casings still warm through their gloves. The air held that tang of cordite that makes a man believe anything's possible for thirty minutes.

"Not bad," the gun captain allowed, which from him might as well have been a love sonnet.

"Gunners satisfied?" the XO asked from the bridge.

"Gunners eating their supper with smiles," came back from the phone talker.

"Good. We'll do it again after lunch until it's boring."

"What if it already is, sir?" Jensen muttered near Mason's ear.

"Then you're finally learning," Mason said, surprising himself with how right it sounded coming out of his mouth.

They secured the gun with a swiftness that would have impressed an admiral and slid back below, the boat shedding topside men like a seal shedding water. Control took the weight of them, the space compressing and somehow feeling bigger at once because it was *theirs*.

"Second gunnery evolution in one hour," the captain said, checking his watch. "Forward room will reset tubes. Engine room, I want charge discipline to the amp."

"Aye," the engine chief answered, the tone of a man who wore the battery like a vest.

The afternoon fell into its usual habits. Surface, fire three at slow count, correct, fire two; down, approach, breath-count, up, match-and-shoot. The tug did his patient dog's work hauling back exercise heads, probably counting each fish like rent from sailors who would never cut him an even check. The destroyer puttered in and out to keep their nerves honest with pretend charges, dull little thumps at range that did nothing but remind a man what the violent ones would feel like.

On one pass the swell turned ugly on the right-handers and the gun captain called his own cease before the OOD did, dropping his hand with a shake of the head. "Not wasting steel to prove a lesson," he growled, and Nolan, who had wandered up to watch, nodded once and carried that approval away as if it were a message the gun crew hadn't needed to hear to keep doing right.

In the forward room Mason got drafted on the line for a time, sweating through the ritual of door checks, drain discipline, and gyro setting under the torpedoman's second class who had three opinions about everything and a soft way with the fish.

"Love 'em and they'll love you back," the man said, patting the sleek cylinder, then caught himself and glanced around. "Don't quote me. Chief'll have my hide for talking like a poet."

"He already does," Mason said. "Just not about torpedoes."

At one point, third submerged run, sun a low gold through the scope, the destroyer guard cut in tighter than his earlier lazy circles and the sound man's voice took on that extra layer men get when math becomes danger. "Guard crossing fast. Bearing one-seven-nine, range eighteen hundred and, Jesus, closing."

Nolan's head turned, not quick, but precise. The captain didn't look around; he looked down at the plot. "Hold your shot," he said mildly. "Let the dog clear his own tail." He waited a beat longer than Mason's breath liked and then said, "Now. Three, FIRE."

The tug's sled clanged obligingly downrange, bong, bong, and the guard destroyer motored by with a grumpy roll that sent spray like tinsel off a Christmas tree. Mason realized he'd set his jaw hard enough to ache and made himself flex it, feeling the heat creep out of his ears. Nolan's knuckles on the periscope column were pale. He blew out through his nose and the color came back.

"Good manners," Nolan said mildly. "The captain, not the tin can."

"Felt close," Mason admitted.

"It wasn't. That's why I like him."

They topped off the afternoon with one last surface shoot in a sunset so ridiculous even the OOD let himself look at it. The three-inch boomed twice, then twice again, and the buoy took it like a professional. The last round rang the target's steel with a sound that came back to the boat thin and pretty as if from very far away.

"Secure from gunnery," the captain said. "We'll make San Diego tomorrow if the world remains this polite. Rig for night running."

Night laid itself down soft as a blanket. Stars crowded the sky. The boat rode a slope of black silk two feet tall and very long. Men went back to the jobs that made the ship breathe: oiling, wiping, listening; plotting, checking, listening; cooking, cleaning, listening. Mac's stew held heat like a coal stove; he thumped a bowl in front of Mason and called it love in a language of insults. "Eat this or I'll strap it to your face."

"Thanks, Mac."

"Don't thank me. Thank the cow."

In Control, the captain signed a sheet that had more holes than words and handed it to the XO. "Log it as routine. Tug and destroyer will send compliments to the tender, I expect."

"Compliments make the coffee better," the XO said dryly.

"Only if Mac lets them."

Mason wandered through the after battery, the smell a familiar cocktail of rubber, acid, and men. He checked a vent flap because he could and found it right. He looked at a cable run because a yard man had touched it yesterday and figured that was reason enough to touch it today. He didn't think about three hundred feet except once, briefly, and it came not like a knife in the gut but like seeing a scar in a mirror, you notice, you nod, you move on.

Nolan found him at the base of the ladder, hands in his jumper pockets, that thin smile. "You look less stupid than you did last month."

"Progress," Mason said. "Chief."

"You know what the boat's going to do before she does it now?"

"Mostly."

"Good. Tomorrow the captain's going to have you stand in for the forward torpedo mate on one run. You'll carry the fire order and you'll own the tube for five minutes. You don't get to be scared. You can be tired, hungry, itchy, or madly in love with Hollywood actresses; none of those matter. Scared is a waste of a man."

Mason swallowed, felt the dryness in his throat, wished he'd stolen another cup of coffee, and said, "Aye."

Nolan started to walk away, then turned back. "And hold your shoulders like you weren't born yesterday. Men look at you before they look at gauges. If you look wrong, they'll feel wrong."

Mason lifted his shoulders a shade. It felt foolish for a heartbeat, then true.

"Better," Nolan said, and went away to make some other man's day harder.

He stood a few minutes longer, letting the boat print its rhythm through his feet into shins, into knees, into the muscles that had stopped fighting her weeks ago. The hum came up the ladder, down the pipes, through the deck, a speech he could now read without words. He closed his eyes and could tell, with a stupid little burst of pleasure, when the planesman trimmed a fraction and when the engine room chief spoiled the motors for the sake of the batteries' happiness.

We're a machine that knows it is one, he thought, and filed the poetry under *things Nolan must never hear me say.*

They were up before dawn, boats always are, even when clocks say otherwise. The tug was a smudge; the destroyer sniffed around as if it had lost a scent. The ocean lay flattish, the kind of morning that makes ship photographers earn their pay.

"Final submerged run," the captain said. "Two fish, then we turn for home."

Mason slid into the forward room like he belonged there and took the spot the torpedo mate pointed to. The tubes loomed like quiet cannons, hatches smooth with oil, dogs seated and safety-cabled. Men moved with the deferential hush people use in churches and engine rooms.

"You carry the captain's fire," the mate said, tapping Mason's chest with two fingers. "You repeat it exactly. Your mouth is nothing else for thirty seconds but a wire. Got it?"

"Got it."

"Don't grin. It's bad luck."

He smoothed his face to neutral and waited.

"Flood one and two," came control's voice through the speaker.

"Flooding one and two," the mate repeated. He glanced to Mason.

Mason put his mouth to the speaking tube and said, evenly, "Flooding one and two." Pressure climbed, held. "Equalized. One and two flooded."

"Open outer doors one and two," came next.

The mate looked, nodded. Mason relayed, "Outer doors open one and two."

"Stand by... Match bearings..."

Mason pressed his palm to the rim of the tube door, a stupid gesture he'd picked up from men who didn't admit to gestures, and felt the cold bite. He told himself it was to ground nerves, not to pray.

", and shoot."

The captain's voice sounded completely bored, which was either genius or cruelty. Mason swallowed. "Tube one, fire."

The mate pulled the lever with a smooth politeness. The boat shifted. "One away."

"Tube two, fire."

The second lever. The hiss, the not-sound of a torpedo choosing a different home than theirs. "Two away."

The room held its collective breath. Far away, through steel and distance and water and wish, the sled said *hello* twice. The mate let out the breath he'd held and clapped Mason on the shoulder once, just bone to bone, no show.

"Didn't break anything," the mate said. "That's the job."

Mason found that his smile came but didn't try to climb off his face. It sat there, tidy and private. He touched the cool steel again with the back of his fingers and stepped away, already making space for the next man to do the exact right thing.

They came up at midmorning to a sky that couldn't decide if it wanted to be kind. Low cloud to the south, bright gaps to the west, the world taking a breath before deciding on weather. The tug waved his last thank-you with the only hand he had, a white rag on a pole. The destroyer tossed a two-flag hoist that meant GOOD SPORT and turned his nose to some other schoolyard.

"Secure from exercises," the captain said, the smallest lift to his syllables. "Set course south, standard speed. We'll be in San Diego tomorrow afternoon if nothing breaks our stride."

"Nothing ever does," Jensen said softly, as if daring fate.

"Shut up," O'Hara and three other men said together, automatic and loving.

On the bridge, Mason stood his turn with the lanyard snug and the horizon long. The three-inch sat clean and smug on its mount, the barrel hot and content. The deck was salted with little brass fingerprints where casings had danced. Far off, a whale threw up a plume that hung like a thought longer than it should have.

Nolan came up into the wind, tugged his cap brim down, and said nothing for a while. Then, "You carried the fire well."

"I tried not to be scared," Mason admitted.

"You can be scared," Nolan said. "You just can't act scared. There's a difference. You had the right one." He let that hang, then added, "You're close."

"Close to what?"

Nolan didn't look at him. "Close." He had a way of trimming words to the weight they could bear. "We'll talk about it tomorrow."

Mason didn't have to ask what *it* was. The word had weight and shape and the polish of a dozen thumbs. He looked south where the coast made a long gray promise and felt his chest do the thing it had learned to do only recently: match the boat.

Behind them, the ocean closed its ledger on another day of men pretending to shoot at things and learning how to actually do it. Ahead, San Diego sat with its quiet harbor and its petty tyrannies and its tender and its bars and its shore patrol and its long rope to the next chapter.

Pike ran easy, the diesels a confidence instead of a threat. Her teeth were sharp and her stomach steady. The men inside her were beginning to act like they'd been born to steel and not soil.

And the sea, indifferent and immense, let them pass.

The sun came up behind the coastal hills like it had been waiting for them. *Pike* ran easy at twelve knots, diesels drumming steady, the sea flat as hammered tin. Land lay off the port beam, a pale green line, low and familiar. The chart said San Clemente Channel, but to the men aboard it meant home.

"San Diego by fourteen hundred if we don't break anything," the XO said, squinting into binoculars.

"Let's not test our luck," the captain replied, and went below.

Mason stood on the bridge wing with Nolan, the wind snapping at their collars. The sky was clear, gulls wheeling high and indifferent. He could taste the difference in the air, land salt, softer, almost sweet. The long run was nearly over.

"Been a while since we came home with everything working," Nolan said.

Mason grinned. "Feels strange."

"Don't worry. The Navy'll fix that soon enough."

They shared a quiet laugh, the kind that comes from shared danger, then settled into silence. *Pike*'s deck gleamed where seawater had washed her clean. Her paint was scuffed, her fittings worn, but she moved like she was proud of herself.

Below, the galley clattered to life, Mac banging pans and cursing at a burner that never did behave. Coffee percolated strong enough to melt spoons. The sound drifted up the hatch, joined by the faint hum of a gramophone someone had smuggled aboard. The tune was slow and scratchy, a dancehall number from another world.

"Never thought I'd miss that noise," Mason said.

"You're learning," Nolan replied. "You miss the racket when it's gone."

By early afternoon, the horizon sharpened. The headlands north of Point Loma stood out clear, and beyond them, the faint line of the San Diego breakwater. Sunlight flashed off the city's windows like signal mirrors. For a moment, even the old hands stopped talking.

"Helm, bring her right to zero-eight-zero," the XO ordered. "We'll come in from the north, standard speed."

The captain appeared topside, hands behind his back, cap brim low. He took in the coastline for a long moment, then said simply, "It's good to see her again."

"Sir," Nolan said, "permission to start topside clean-up once we hit the lane?"

"Granted."

Mason and the others went to work without needing direction, coiling lines, wiping salt, securing hatches for in-port. They moved with the easy precision of men who knew every sound, every step. No shouted orders, no wasted motion.

The signal bridge called down, "Tender reports pier four clear, sir. *Holland* is inboard."

Nolan gave a soft whistle. "Back where we started."

Mason looked up at the red brick buildings and the cranes on the tender's deck. "Feels like years ago."

"It was," Nolan said. "For you, anyway."

As *Pike* eased through the channel, tugs appeared, stubby and purposeful, throwing up rooster tails of foam. The harbor air changed, diesel exhaust mixing with tar, oil, and the faint tang of fish. Familiar, grounding smells. The breakwater slid by, the sea fell flat, and the city opened ahead like a promise.

"Engines ahead one-third," the captain ordered. "Helm, steady on the buoy line. Let's bring her home looking like we know how."

At the pier, a small crowd waited, officers from the tender, a few yard men, and a handful of sailors in liberty whites who had the easy grin of men about to spend pay. A photographer stood ready with a box camera. The tugs nudged *Pike* into position; lines went over; cleats clanged.

"All stop," the captain said. "Secure engines."

The diesels wound down with a final, throaty sigh. For a moment, silence reigned, the strange quiet of arrival. Then orders started again, and the world picked up its rhythm.

Mason coiled the last line, wiped his hands, and looked up at the tender looming alongside. The same gray hulk, the same smell of paint and hot metal. But it wasn't the same to him anymore.

"Welcome home, boys!" a voice called from the pier. "Didn't drown, I see."

O'Hara yelled back, "We tried, but the boat wouldn't let us!"

Laughter rolled down the deck. Even the captain smiled.

That evening, after lines were secured and watches set, the crew gathered in the forward battery compartment. The air was thick with heat and the smell of oil and coffee. The captain stood beneath a low lamp, a sheet of orders in one hand and a small velvet box in the other.

"Before we all scatter to liberty," he said, "there's one bit of business to attend to."

Nolan stepped forward from the crowd. "Machinist's Mate Third Class Daniel Mason, front and center."

Mason blinked, then stood quickly, heart hammering. He'd known it was coming, maybe even suspected this was why Nolan had been watching him so closely the last week, but hearing it out loud still made his palms sweat.

He stepped into the narrow space before the captain, the low ceiling making the moment oddly intimate.

"During the last patrol cycle," the captain said, "this man has demonstrated the skill, endurance, and awareness expected of a qualified submariner. His boat reports him ready."

Nolan nodded once. "He's ready, sir."

The captain opened the velvet box. Inside, gleaming even under the dim light, lay a small set of silver dolphins.

"Mason," the captain said, "you've earned these, not by memorizing manuals, but by knowing this boat, her systems, and her soul. That's what makes a submariner."

He pinned the dolphins to Mason's jumper, the metal cold against his chest.

"Congratulations. You're one of us now."

The compartment erupted in applause, not loud, but heartfelt. Men clapped shoulders, shouted quiet congratulations. O'Hara grinned like a proud brother. Jensen whistled low and said, "About damn time."

Mason didn't trust his voice. He just nodded and said, "Thank you, sir. Thank you, Chief."

Nolan stepped close enough that only Mason heard him. "Wear 'em honest. The steel will know if you don't."

Mason smiled. "Aye, Chief."

By sunset, the shipyard lights along the bay blinked to life. The crew filed across the gangway in small groups, liberty passes in hand, shoes polished, uniforms clean. The MPs at the landing checked each man with that practiced suspicion unique to shore patrol. A few men saluted, a few didn't. It was all the same ritual.

Mason lingered by the rail before crossing. The tender loomed tall above, cranes idle, deck lights glowing soft. The air was heavy with the smell of oil, salt, and home.

"Not going ashore?" Nolan asked, appearing beside him.

"In a bit," Mason said. "Just wanted a minute."

"Good instinct. Most men run off too quick and forget to say thank you."

Mason looked down at the deck plates, then back at the Chief. "You really think she'd know?"

"I don't think. I know." Nolan leaned on the rail. "You'll find that out soon enough. Boats remember who listens and who doesn't."

"I'll remember."

"You better. The next boat won't be as forgiving."

Mason frowned. "Next boat?"

Nolan nodded toward the tender. "Scuttlebutt says orders are coming down. We're bound west soon. Pearl Harbor, maybe farther."

Mason felt a thrill under the fatigue. "The Asiatic Fleet?"

"Could be. That's where the sharp boys are going. The captain's itching for it."

Mason looked out across the harbor, the faint outlines of other submarines, the city lights beyond. "Guess we won't be staying here long."

"No sailor ever does."

They stood there a moment longer, the hum of the generators filling the space between them. Then Nolan clapped him on the shoulder. "Go. Have a drink. Spend your pay before someone finds a way to take it."

Mason grinned. "Aye, Chief."

Later, after most of the crew had gone ashore, Mason walked the pier alone. The night was cool and still. The water lapped softly against the pilings, reflecting the pier lights in broken streaks of gold. The *Holland*'s massive shadow loomed beside *Pike*, cranes jutting like fingers into the night sky.

From somewhere down the line came laughter, sailors already half drunk, voices echoing over the quiet water. Farther out, the faint chug of a harbor tug marked time like a heartbeat.

He stopped beside the boat and looked down at her from the pier. She seemed smaller now, resting quietly against the fenders. Yet in his mind, he could still feel the weight of the ocean pressing against her hull, hear the hum of her motors, the groan of her steel. The living, breathing boat that had taken him down and brought him back.

His hand brushed the dolphins on his chest. They were cool now, but they carried their own warmth, the kind that didn't come from metal, but from meaning.

"She's something, isn't she?" a voice said behind him.

Mason turned. It was the captain, cap under his arm, cigarette glowing faintly in the dark.

"Yes, sir," Mason said. "She is."

"Good patrol," the captain said. "You did well."

"Thank you, sir."

"Next time'll be different," the captain said quietly. "Deeper water. Longer runs. Things are changing fast out west."

"Yes, sir."

The captain drew on his cigarette, the ember flaring red. "Get your rest, Mason. We'll need all the hands we can get before long."

He walked away toward the tender, leaving Mason alone with the hum of the harbor.

Mason stayed there a while longer, watching the reflection of the city lights dance on the rippling water.

Out beyond the breakwater, the Pacific stretched dark and infinite, a silent invitation.

He thought about the drills, the dives, the tests, and the way the boat had felt alive under his feet. He thought about Nolan's words: Boats remember who listens.

He smiled, touching the silver dolphins again, then turned toward the gangway.

Tomorrow would bring new orders, maybe even a new ocean. But tonight, the boat was home.

And for the first time since he'd left the farm, he felt like he belonged exactly where he was, beneath the waves, inside the living heart of steel.

Chapter 9

Orders from the Pacific

The harbor stirred before dawn, a low murmur of engines and gulls echoing through the mist. Tugboats moved like shadows, their stacks puffing white ghosts across the still water. Along Pier Four, *Pike* waited, hull gleaming, decks scrubbed, her fresh gray paint glistening under dew. She looked proud, alive.

The tender *Holland* loomed beside her, cranes creaking as crates of stores and torpedoes swung aboard, like a mother feeding her restless child. Steam curled upward and vanished in the half-light.

The captain stood on the pier, clipboard under his arm, watching every motion with the tight patience of a man whose mind was already at sea. "Orders are confirmed," he said to Nolan and the XO. "Pearl first, then forward assignment. Pacific Fleet wants us sharp, there's talk of long patrols before year's end."

Nolan's face was unreadable. "We'll be ready, sir."

"We are ready," the captain said, eyes glinting. "Let's make it official."

By eight bells, the crew was mustered, white hats lined in the morning chill, liberty passes turned in, seabags at their feet. A brass trio from the tender struck up a crooked version of "Anchors Aweigh," the notes drifting out over diesel fumes and salt.

Mason stood amid the ranks, seabag slung over his shoulder, dolphins catching the faint sunlight. The air smelled of oil, seaweed, and paint, the perfume of his new world.

Nolan paced the line, sharp-eyed and steady. "Check your tags, your gear, and your mouths. If you forgot something, it's gone now."

O'Hara muttered, "What if I forgot my luck?"

"Then borrow Jensen's," Nolan shot back. "He's got more than he deserves."

Laughter rippled through the ranks. Even the captain's mouth twitched before he barked, "Stations for getting underway."

Lines came in. The tug edged forward, water swirling brown against the pilings. On the pier, a few officers saluted as *Pike* eased away.

Engines coughed, caught, and settled into their heartbeat rhythm. The vibration came up through the soles of Mason's boots, steady, living, familiar. The pier slid away until only the echo of gulls remained.

San Diego receded, cranes and hills melting into the pale sky. Mason stood topside with his section, spray cool on his face. The same city that had once felt vast now looked small, toy-like, a memory already fading.

"Feels different this time," he said.

Nolan nodded beside him. "Because you're not leaving home anymore. You're taking it with you."

Mason understood. The *Pike* was home now, hot, noisy, alive, unpredictable.

By afternoon, the coastline blurred to gray, and the Pacific opened wide and calm. The rhythm of the boat steadied, her motion smooth and easy. Mason leaned against the coaming, binoculars resting on his chest. The sea glittered, endless, beautiful, indifferent.

"You can tell a good crew," Nolan said, "by how quiet the deck is."

Mason smiled. "And how loud the galley."

"That too."

The captain came up for air, surveying the horizon. "Every voyage feels like a beginning," he said quietly. "But the sea remembers everything."

As dusk settled, the world turned copper and rose. The mess crew brought coffee topside, against regulation but with the captain's silent blessing. O'Hara's harmonica played low, sweet, tired. Even the old man smiled.

When the last light sank, Mason lingered at the rail. The stars blinked awake, so sharp they looked like holes punched through heaven. Somewhere far below, the boat's heartbeat thrummed through the steel.

He wrote another letter that night, not to be mailed, just to steady his hands.

> Dear Mom,
> I'm heading west again, farther this time. The boat moves, and you move with her. She breathes, and you learn to breathe with her. I think I was meant for this life.
> Love, Dan

He folded the paper carefully and slipped it into his locker, marked "To Be Mailed in Port."

Sleep came uneasy. The hum of machinery filled the compartments, the air warm with diesel and sweat. Mason dreamed of water, endless, quiet, rising over fields that turned into steel.

At dawn, he climbed to the bridge for morning watch. The horizon burned soft gold, the Pacific like glass. The captain stood by the shears, hands clasped behind his back.

"Beautiful morning," he said.

"Yes, sir."

He smiled faintly. "Every patrol starts like this. Clean. Full of promise. It never lasts."

Mason's voice was steady. "Feels right, sir. Feels like she's alive."

"She is," the captain said. "You take care of her, she'll take care of you."

They watched the sun climb higher, painting the deck in light. Mason thought of the letter, of home, of the strange peace that came only when submerged.

Then the intercom crackled: "Bridge, Radio. Priority message from COMSUBPAC. Immediate delivery."

The captain frowned, took the slip from the runner, and read in silence. His face hardened.

"New orders," he said finally. "Unidentified contact reported off Point Conception. A destroyer returning to San Diego picked it up, possible submarine. No surface sighting, but their hydrophones caught something... irregular."

A pause. The sea rolled gentle around them.

"Plot course two-one-zero. Dive the boat."

The klaxon wailed. "Dive, dive!"

Mason moved without thought, dogging hatches, securing lines, watching as the sunlight narrowed, dimmed, and vanished. Water surged over the hull, green fading to black. Gauges twitched. The ballast tanks rumbled.

At one hundred feet, the world went still. Only the hum of

motors and the faint sigh of pressure filled the control room.

Then, a sound.

Faint, distant. Three slow pulses through the hull. Pause. Then three again.

Mason froze, hand on the steel. "Chief... you hear that?"

Nolan turned, eyes sharp. "She's breathing," Mason whispered.

"Not her," Nolan said. "Listen."

The sound came again, deeper now, almost like a heartbeat echoing from miles away. It wasn't mechanical. It wasn't their engines. It was *outside*.

The captain's voice was low. "Helm, steady at depth. Hold position."

They waited. Nothing but silence.

Finally, the captain said, "All ahead one-third. Let's see what's down here."

As *Pike* crept forward, the sea pressed close, black and infinite. Mason felt the vibration in his bones, not just from the boat, but from the deep itself.

He whispered without realizing it, "She's not the only one alive down here."

Nolan gave a quiet nod. "No, son. The ocean's waking up."

Mason looked at the depth gauge, the needle steady at

150 feet. He thought of his letter, of the words he hadn't written: *Sometimes, Mom, it feels like the sea is listening.*

Above them, the surface shimmered with sunlight they'd already left behind. Below, the dark seemed endless, patient, waiting.

And somewhere out there, in that vast, unseen world, something stirred and listened back.

About the Dolphins

The Submarine Warfare Insignia, known simply as "dolphins", was first authorized in 1924. The emblem shows a submarine from the bow flanked by two dolphins, ancient guardians of sailors and symbols of command of the sea. To wear them is to be "Qualified in Submarines," a title earned only through knowledge, endurance, and the trust of one's shipmates.

Qualification is no small thing. It can take a year or more of study, drills, and tests, and a man must know every system aboard, air, water, engines, valves, circuits. He must prove he can fight fires, stop flooding, and save the boat when all else fails. Only when the crew agrees he can be trusted with their lives does he earn his place among them.

To those who have never served, the dolphins may seem a simple pin. To those who have, they are far more, a symbol of courage, mastery, and quiet pride. In the cramped heat and noise of a submarine, where a single mistake can kill all hands, they become a badge of belonging, a promise that each man knows his duty and will not fail the others who depend on him.

Author's Note

While *The Living Boat* takes place within the real world of the United States Navy in the years leading up to World War II, this story is first and foremost a work of fiction.

The boats, ports, and routines described are inspired by history, but the people who inhabit them, Daniel Mason, Chief Noland, and their shipmates, are products of imagination, meant to honor the spirit of the submariners who lived and served in that era.

I've tried to keep the story true to the times: the technology, the training, and the rhythm of life aboard an early diesel submarine. Some names, locations, and timelines have been adapted for narrative flow. My intent wasn't to recreate exact events, but to capture the feeling of those years, the uncertainty, the brotherhood, and the strange bond between man, machine, and the sea.

Any errors or liberties taken are my own, and I hope readers will forgive them in favor of the story's heart.

Acknowledgments

I want to thank everyone I served with during my years in the United States Navy. The memories, lessons, and friendships from those days shaped not only this story, but the way I see the world. Your professionalism, humor, and courage under pressure continue to inspire me.

A special thank you to my parents for always encouraging curiosity and determination, even when my goals seemed out of reach. And to my wife, whose patience, support, and belief in this project gave me the time and space to bring *The Living Boat* to life, none of this would have been possible without you.

Continue the Journey

Daniel Mason's story continues in

Book Two of *The Silent Depths Series*

Beneath the Rising Sun

The calm of peacetime fades as the *USS Pike* sails west across the Pacific. Whispers of war grow louder, alliances shift, and Mason finds himself facing not only the vastness of the sea but the coming storm of history. New challenges, old rivalries, and the first taste of combat will test everything he's learned, and everything he believes about courage and survival.

Continue the journey with the rest of The Silent Depths series, available on Amazon as each book is released.

Coming Soon — 2026

About the Author

Eric Hawley, MMCS(SS), USN (Ret)

Served in the United States Navy from 1991 to 2013 as a nuclear machinist's mate aboard the submarines *USS Florida*, *USS Jefferson City*, and *USS Hampton*. His years beneath the sea shaped his deep respect for the men who lived and worked in that silent world, a brotherhood few ever see but never forget.

Drawing on those experiences, he writes *The Silent Depths* series to capture not only the history of submarine warfare, but the humanity of those who served, their courage, fear, humor, and endurance.

When he's not writing, Eric works as a consultant and engineer and builds live steam model locomotives, blending his love of precision engineering with hands-on craftsmanship. He lives in Snohomish, Washington with his family. *The Living Boat* is his first novel.